PRAISE FOR KENNETH STEVEN'S WRITING:

'Kenneth Steven has a ready sensitivity to the beauty of small moments.'
The Herald

'There is a grave beauty in these lines, revealing a poetic voice of great sensitivity.'
Alexander McCall Smith

'Kenneth has a rare gift of being able to transmute the mundane into the mesmerizing, in a kind of poetic alchemy.'
Countryman

'Here is poetry of rare honesty, touching on the vital needs of the spirit in our age and manifesting a profound awareness of and concern for the world about us.'
John F Deane

'Has a talent for capturing the startling, original image ... he is a fine, fine poet'
New Shetlander

Published by Saraband,
Suite 202, 98 Woodlands Road,
Glasgow, G3 6HB,
Scotland

www.saraband.net

10 9 8 7   6 5 4 3 2 1

ISBN: 9781910192559
ISBNe: 9781910192566

Typeset by Iolaire Typography Ltd.
Printed and bound in Great Britain by Clays Ltd, St Ives plc.

2020 is entirely a work of fiction, and all the characters
are products of the author's imagination.

A NOVEL

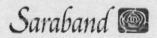

★

I USED TO see them, yes. They were a polite group; I couldn't say anything other than that. Always sat together as a foursome; would sometimes stay until the place closed. I remember once having to chase them out. I would say it was one of the boys that was the most talkative; I haven't a clue what his name was or what any of them were called. I think someone else described them to me as animated. That's not a word I would ever use, but I suppose it would be right. The girl was probably the quietest, at least from what I saw. When I was working behind the counter I'd glance up at them from time to time and she'd be listening. She was pretty.

I can feel only sorrow in the light of what's happened. Oh, you don't want me to mention that – all right. Well, there's really nothing more to say than that. I saw them now and again; I found them friendly enough to deal with, and I don't think I ever gave them a second thought. I mean, it's a multi-cultural community we're living in. You take that for granted and don't question it. In my childhood you were surprised if you saw a black or

Asian face, but I was growing up in rural England. This is Manchester, and I dare say Manchester has been this way for a hundred years. No, I saw nothing out of the ordinary, nothing to make me suspicious. I'm sorry to be unhelpful, but I can't say more than that.

★

'LET US TURN to something allied to the subject, and I'm actually going to be speaking to an individual who has asked not to be identified. I think it's likely that the line will be poor, and I can only apologise for that in advance, but let's see how we get on. We should say that our speaker is in the north of England – that much we can reveal. And you have agreed to speak to us – indeed you *wanted* to speak to us – regarding Sharia law?'

'Yes.'

'Do please go on.'

'Well, I have been concerned for some time now.'

'And I believe that you are aware of Sharia law being implemented?'

'Oh, yes. I would say I know of the existence of at least five Sharia law courts. They are moving around all the time so as not to get caught, and they are dealing with cases in each place.'

'When you say *cases*, what exactly do you mean?'

'I mean theft, I mean adultery, I mean even cases of murder.'

'And why are they being dealt with by such courts? Is it because it is felt British justice is simply not effective?'

'Yes, not effective, and not sufficiently severe. British prisons are full of convicts who will come out and re-offend. There is very little sense of justice, very little sense that those who have been wronged have been compensated, that those who have committed crimes have been punished. This is a way of ensuring that crime is dealt with.'

'And can I ask about punishments? There have been stories that seem to suggest punishments can be very severe – the cutting off of a hand, for example, or imprisonment in cells that have been created for the use of solitary confinement.'

'No, I would not want to comment on that. I think you would have to speak to someone much closer to the Sharia courts. I am aware only of their existence and of how they are operated.'

'Well, can I ask you about something else our programme has been discussing in the past few days, and that is female genital mutilation? Can you tell us if these courts have jurisdiction over FGM? Have they had a direct involvement in the use of FGM in this country?'

'Well, there is not direct involvement.'

'But would these courts be in any way responsible for the carrying out of female genital mutilation? Would they at some level be concerned with arranging the cutting of girls?'

(The line goes dead.)

'Well, we seem to have lost our speaker at an unfortunate moment, and in a way that poses as many questions as it answers…'

★

Prime Minister's Question Time:

'Will he at the very least admit the situation in this country is out of control? This week, police in the Sudburgh area – and we now know this is just one of several places in the north of England – have effectively given up. There are communities beyond the rule of law, where in fact we do not know what is going on. Does he not accept that this is an untenable situation and that it is time a task force was established to take back control of each and every one of these communities?'

'All I would say by reply is this – which party is governing in the vast majority of these areas? I would say that it's the leader of the opposition's responsibility to get his house in order and ensure that he has jurisdiction over elements of his party that are out of control! In fact, I think it's time he went down to some of these town halls himself – if he's got the courage – and started knocking a few heads together! It's not me he should be hectoring; it's his own representatives who obviously don't have a clue what their own leader is saying. Perhaps that says something about the lack of control he has, but it's not for me to lie awake at night worrying about that: it's for him!'

'The Prime Minister knows full well that his party is in government and that trying to pass the buck cannot and will not work. And in answer to such a cheap political jibe, I will respond by saying that I have very much been in some of these constituencies over the course of the past seven days. The problems in these communities transcend the political divide, and cheap attempts to dump the problems onto the opposition are not acceptable. It's time that he got out of the Westminster Bubble and into some of the hot water! Earlier this week one of his own members of parliament said, and I quote, "Six more months of this and the place is going to be on fire. All it will take is the striking of a match in the wrong place, and my fear is for those who are going to get burned." How much clearer can the message be? Maybe as well as being deaf to warnings like that from those within his own party, he's blind to what's being written in every serious paper in the land this week. Perhaps he should get out a bit more. But in the light of what his own member of parliament warned, can I strongly advise that he wear fire-resistant clothing!'

★

WE WERE FRIGHTENED. I think things began to get worse during the May of that year. It seemed to be that the racist message became louder, even that it was deemed more acceptable. I had very seldom known racist abuse in the shop – in fact, it was more often the opposite. When my wife and I first opened the shop in the 1950s we were welcomed, and not only by other members of the Pakistani community. Plenty of white neighbours came in and wished us well, too. There was nothing but friendliness. Over the years there were a few times we had problems, but mostly it was because I think we were vulnerable in the very middle of the town. Groups of drunken young men going home late on a Saturday night: once or twice I was shouted at, things were shoved through the letterbox. Once somebody wrote something on the front door, but we were almost amused: they couldn't even spell Pakistani correctly! So I would say that what we experienced was nothing compared to the past few months – perhaps the past year.

My daughter began to be frightened. She is married with her own young child, and she noticed the change. It wasn't just comments or the shouting on a Saturday night. It was bricks through the windows, and one went into her daughter's bedroom. The child was terrified. When you are inside a room and a brick comes through the window it is truly terrifying. She wanted to leave. She wanted to move out as soon as possible so her family was safe. But where was she to go? This is where she grew up; it is where her own family lives and the members of her community. For her husband it is no different. He works in the town and his extended family is close by. My granddaughter has her two families close to her. But they are afraid to let her out of their sight. They are concerned about what it will be like when she goes to school. This makes me angry. We have never done anything to cause trouble in this country. We have lived quiet lives and worked hard, and suddenly we have to be afraid of everything we do. This is unfair. We are not the extremists that they hate. Why should we be made to feel guilty? I am sorry to be emotional but I cannot help it. I am both sad and angry, because there is nothing I can do. There is nothing any of us can do and it does not have to be this way. It should not be this way. I only see things becoming worse. I do not know where it will end and I am afraid – I feel truly frightened.

★

I REMEMBER THE four of them. Well, I remember three of them – I saw the girl only once or twice. When I think now about what happened it is hard to believe it could have been them, the same people. They were kids. That is the truth of it – they were nothing more than kids.

Earnest talking: those are the words that come to mind at once. But I don't think that even now I can assume their talk was malevolent, plotting. The truth is that I can't know; none of us can know. They were friends; there was nothing about this particular group of four that stood out. Perhaps the one boy. It is dangerous to read too much into everything in hindsight, but one of the boys seemed almost to be the leader. I remember him walking past my desk one day in the library and we glanced at each other. Except with him it was more than a glance. I know that at that second I felt there was something about his eyes. I even remember thinking about it afterwards, asking myself if my thinking was racist. As perhaps all of us have done in recent years, asked ourselves about our own motives and our attitudes. Was it his particular look or was it his ethnic origin? Was I prejudiced against a look we might call Islamist? There is no such thing, but we have almost come to think there is. How many of us white Caucasians have stood waiting to board a flight and seen that face ahead of us in the queue? And the thought has gone through us – just the flash of a thought. Are they safe? Are they really boarding that plane, our plane, for the same reason as us? And we castigate ourselves for even asking the question, at the same time as asking it all the same. We have created our idea of an Islamist face, for better or worse.

So I stamped their books; no doubt I exchanged the odd word with them too. But I did not know them. I had no reason to know them and I had no reason to be suspicious of them. I felt prejudice against that one boy, that one young man, for what may be nothing more than my own in-built and built-up resentment. Perhaps it is true to say that I felt he looked at me that morning with a kind of defiance. Perhaps I did feel there was fire in his eyes; it's certainly true that his look shocked me somehow. I see hundreds of students every day; I know one or two by name, but the vast majority are little more than faces to me. There is no interaction; there is no need to know more. Many do not even meet your eye when you look at them. Perhaps it was that seeming determination to meet my eye, that wish almost to intimidate, that I could not forget – that set me thinking. But I know nothing for certain. I cannot tell the difference, then or now, between what I saw and what I might have imagined I saw.

★

Yes, I remember Eric Semple, but I will say from the outset that I did not know him well. I was at school with him; all the way through primary and up until we would have been fourteen, fifteen. My parents moved away with us to Leeds when I was fifteen: perfect timing, just when I was working for my most important exams.

But I stress that I did not know Eric Semple well. I was never at his house; I never met any of his family. There's another ten or twelve you could have interviewed today who would have known him to the same degree as I did, and probably better. I suppose if there was anything there was a kind of circle. And he did attract people. I think it's almost impossible to say what it was. I suppose he must have had something about him, but I don't think for the life of me I could tell you what it was.

Well, we were all teenage boys – perhaps it was as simple as that. Eric was very much a boys' boy: he was very *masculine*, if I can say that. If there was a risk that could be taken, he was up for it. In fact, one of that group was actually injured at some point; I can't recall what it was we were doing. But there was a lot of crossing of railway lines and climbing into places. He wasn't particularly strong and there were others who were tougher, but Eric inspired. I can imagine someone suggesting some new idea and his eyes flashing. He had a kind of goodness of heart that made him likeable – and that almost made you want him to like you.

But if you crossed him you were for it. He had a flash of temper that took you by surprise. He seemed too placid for that – just too nice. I reckon all of us got him wrong on that. I remember him laying into one of us for having gone behind his back. The anger just came from nowhere. It diminished quickly, too, but it just lit like a flame.

The only incident I knew about – but didn't witness

– happened after I had moved. Perhaps just weeks after we went to Leeds. Eric and three of the others in our circle were out late one Saturday night. Whether they deliberately went into the district or whether they met the gang by accident I don't know. I remember the whole thing being in the papers; it might even have made it onto television, but I'm not sure now. At any rate, they ran into a group of Asians and they were outnumbered – possibly by two to one. Eric got a hell of a beating. For whatever reason he was seen as the leader: he may perhaps have shouted something, have taunted them. You had to be careful when he'd been drinking; that anger was even closer to the surface.

He was more or less left for dead. He was strong, and a fighter, but he was beaten to a pulp. I'm sure that had a real effect; I'm not going to deny that. I don't honestly know what he thought before that. We didn't talk politics; I can't recall a single occasion when we did. I'm not honestly sure we were mature enough for that. It was about taking risks and pushing boundaries. But Eric was far brighter than he made out. He was certainly a dark horse. And he worked hard at home, even if he never did at school. And I heard that once he fought his way back after that beating he worked harder still. I don't think any of that group had the slightest ambition to get to university; I'm not sure Eric would have done at that time. I think what happened changed him in a big way. Strangely enough, it may even have knocked a kind of sense into him. But I had lost touch with him by then. I was away and out of his circle by that stage. I'm not the best person to ask, I'm really aware of that. I'm simply not the best person to ask. But he did change, of that I'm absolutely certain. Was it for the better or the worse? I think it all depends what side of the divide you are on.

★

THERE IS GROWING evidence that a breakaway group from the British National Party has joined forces with a section of the English Defence League to form an organisation called White Rose. The splinter group would appear to be composed of discontented members from both organisations intent on creating a much more militant community of activists. It is claimed the two breakaway factions have become more and more dissatisfied with the way their respective organisations have normalised their activities over recent years. White Rose is being described by one source as an army of resistance to waves of immigration past and present, and it seems at least part of the inspiration – and assistance – for the formation of the group may have come from the southern states of America. The police have refused to comment, as has the Home Office, but it is known that there have been severe tensions within the ranks of the British National

Party and the English Defence League in Manchester and Birmingham in particular in recent months. No member of either organisation was willing to comment on these reports, which remain unconfirmed.

★

THE CCTV IMAGES are clear here from Edinburgh Waverley Station. If we freeze this image you can see two of the male suspects leaving the service they have taken from Manchester; we're still uncertain as to why they wanted to board the East Coast Rail service in Edinburgh. It may be that they had plans to meet someone here prior to carrying out the attack; it may be they did in fact meet that person or persons during their time in the city. Otherwise, absolutely predictable behaviour: here you can see them crossing as a group to enter the station precincts proper – the female suspect even turns to laugh with the third of the male suspects immediately prior to entering the building. The important thing to stress is that they come across as absolutely relaxed – carefree even – and that ties in completely with later accounts from the train. The key suspect at this point would seem to be the third male: if you look at this image you can see the large, heavy-looking bag he's carrying. This is where *the device has been concealed. They arrive at Waverley at ten thirty-four pm, and have almost one hour exactly at the station before boarding the King's Cross service at eleven thirty pm. We do lose sight of two of the males for most of the full duration of that hour; the suspect with the device can be followed for the entire time – he simply sits outside the main ticket office and toilet facilities with the bags – and the girl we see intermittently. We don't know what happens to the other two males for that hour: it's more than likely there was a meeting of some kind and we still hope to shed light on this. In the meantime, I'm happy to take questions from the media, but I must stress that it is likely to be a frustrating session. For very obvious reasons, I am not at liberty to divulge certain information as a result of our ongoing inquiries, both for the safety of members of the force and of the public. So when I cannot answer a particular question I would appreciate it if no further attempt is made to gain information. I would remind all of you that this is one of the biggest post-war operations there has been, for very necessary reasons.*

★

I THINK MANY working-class men in particular felt enough was enough. Which party cares about our existence? The Labour Party certainly doesn't: they abandoned the working class a long time ago. They wanted to win over the undecided higher up, and so they became a middle-class party. The unions, the anti-nuclear movement, a whole lot else – all that was sacrificed on the altar. I think many men especially were angry; they felt totally abandoned. Who was representing them? Certainly not the Tories or the Liberals. I felt in a no-man's-land, that's for sure, with no idea who to believe any more. I think a lot of men in particular simply gave up voting altogether. What was the point? If the party wasn't bothered about them, why should they run to defend the party?

I think it was dangerous. It meant a lot of men from traditionally hard-working backgrounds, who weren't getting any better off, were in danger of becoming extremists. They saw Asians and blacks getting free flats and widescreen televisions because they happened to have the right colour of skin. I think political correctness has a lot to answer for. It makes people even angrier; it doesn't solve a thing. You have to educate to do that; creating nice slogans and putting the right faces on television solves nothing at all. It just makes people even more resentful.

And I don't think the race questions were really being looked at. There was a whole lot you couldn't talk about. The fact that it was gangs of black youths that were doing most of the killing in London – you couldn't talk about that. It was never admitted in the media. People aren't stupid, but politicians make them out to be. Political correctness has the opposite effect in my opinion. It causes even more resentment. I don't believe it makes ethnic minorities feel any better about themselves. Probably they feel patronised.

So having something to join was important. It made people, especially men, feel they had something at last. The fact it was radical and ready to act mattered. They were tired of silence and inquiries and political correctness on all sides. This was about marching and about telling the truth. About getting our country back. I'm not sure we hated anybody, not to begin with. We were angry, pure and simple. I don't think it takes a detective to work out where that anger came from. I don't feel ashamed of it. I never have. We believed that what we were doing was for the best. I still believe that. I always will.

★

I HAVE AGREED to talk about my son for one reason only: I am ashamed of him. I never believed that such a thing would be possible, but it is. When you bring a child into this world, when you are a mother especially – how can you feel shame? Love is unconditional: all parents must see their child making mistakes, but they have to forgive again and again. As a Muslim I forgive, but I am ashamed just the same, and I cannot believe that shame will diminish. I had such high hopes for my son; both my husband and I had such high hopes. What do you do with the memories of those hopes when such a thing as this happens? I have to carry the shame of this within my community; the anger comes from both sides – from all sides. And I am not surprised.

It was my parents who came to settle in England from Pakistan, and my husband's parents. You could say our marriage was arranged; perhaps it is better to say it was planned. They were grateful for what they had been given. They did not talk about that much, but I knew it in my father especially. He had a harsh upbringing and coming to England for him was a kind of escape. He carried a gratitude within him that I saw now and again, that I could almost hear in his voice sometimes.

So I feel shame and I also feel guilt. I feel guilt that I did not pass on this sense of gratitude to my son and my daughter. But I am not sure they would have understood what he felt; I am not certain that gratitude would have made any sense to them. My children grew up with everything they needed. They never knew what it meant to go without. In that respect it was no different from how the other children round about them lived.

I blame a virtual world for stealing my son away. We did everything we could to set him on the right road, but how do you bring someone back from a virtual world? Yes, I was aware that I was losing him at the end of his school days. He went to his bedroom at ten o'clock every night, school days and weekends, and I knew he was not sleeping. I knew he was on the computer, but we trusted him never to watch pornography. We were certain that was not an issue.

Yes, he had two friends in particular. He met them in his first year at university and they came a few times to visit. They would always be in his room talking. I never heard laughter from them, just their voices. Sometimes I came upstairs to find something and I heard their voices. They would go quiet as if they knew someone was there outside. Once I knocked and asked if they wanted anything, but my son answered and said they were fine. They were always polite, but my son never introduced them and they always left the house together. He didn't want to talk about them. By then he didn't want to talk about anything. I felt I had lost him. Perhaps that is looking back on it now. I am not sure how much I thought about it then. He still seemed so young, only one year out of school.

I feel shame and guilt, one as much as the other. And I do not know what to do with either of them. I believe I will take them with me to my grave.

★

I SAW THE whole thing as it happened. We live on a farm and the London line is almost exactly a mile west of us. When you're outside you can generally hear the trains going past, if the wind's right especially. You just take them for granted; you get used to them.

I simply got up that night to open the window. It had been very still that day and quite hot. We'd gone to bed and the room was too warm. My partner Kevin suffers from asthma and that kind of airlessness is what he finds almost the worst. I think we'd woken up about twenty minutes earlier and he was wheezing. I got up to open the window and let in some fresher air.

I saw the whole thing, you could say, in slow motion. My eyes were right on it as I heard this colossal bang and the train seemed to light up, turn this orange colour, and the carriages just went this way and that. It's hard to piece it all back together now: you can't tell afterwards how long the whole thing lasted. You're so much in shock, you don't know. I don't know whether I screamed or was silent. I think it was all the stranger, all the more horrible, because after the explosion I don't remember hearing a thing. You just saw the crumpling of all these carriages that were lit up. You imagine afterwards those who must have been inside and the noise there would have been: the absolute terror and the screaming. And I could see it all happening in front of me and not hear a thing. Total silence.

Even now I don't remember a thing. I must have turned away from the window but it was like swimming through deep water. I don't know what I said to Kevin but I could hear myself speaking; I could see him coming towards me and I knew that everything else was forgotten. He was throwing on his clothes to go out there, telling me to do things. It was just a total nightmare, but you do things all the same – you have to. Something else takes over and you do what you have to – I suppose it's what they call automatic pilot. The next thing I remember is being on the phone, but I have no idea how much later that was. I have no earthly idea. I don't think time meant much any more. Every second was cut up into hundreds of little bits, and afterwards you see them all like in a film. That was the way it was.

★

*I*T IS BELIEVED *there was an explosion at just after four thirty this morning on an East Coast sleeper train travelling from Edinburgh to London, which come off the line about sixty miles north of London. At least a hundred and sixty-four passengers are known to have been killed, but it is feared the death toll may rise considerably. There is speculation that a bomb was detonated on board, and the whole area around the crash site is being treated as a crime scene. An emergency meeting of the COBRA defence* team will be held later this morning, and it is understood that the Prime Minister will make a statement when he visits the scene of the crash thereafter. The Archbishop of Canterbury has asked that people 'of all faiths and none' stop what they are doing at some point in the next hours to keep all those who have been killed or injured in their thoughts and prayers. It is believed that a class of primary children who were to be performing at a concert later today in London were among those travelling: it was the first time that some of the youngsters had been away from home on their own. Representatives from all of the political parties have spoken of their utter revulsion at the tragedy, and of their fears that this might have been some kind of terrorist attack. However, no group has claimed any kind of responsibility for the crash, and police are stressing that it will be some hours before any kind of detailed picture of precisely what happened can be given. In the meantime, those anxious about the well-being or relatives or friends are asked to call one of several special numbers set up by East Coast. Those numbers will be given in full at the end of this bulletin, and they are also to be found on our website and on that of East Coast. Extra staff have been drafted in to cope with the expected volume of calls over the coming hours, and East Coast have asked that callers remain patient because of the unprecedented nature of the situation.

Our main headline once more: it is believed there has been an explosion on an East Coast sleeper train, which came off the line at just after four thirty this morning in *open country about sixty miles north of London. There is some speculation that a bomb was detonated on board. The death toll stands at present at a hundred and sixty-four, and there are reports of large numbers of people with serious injuries – especially of passengers who have suffered severe burns. The site of the crash is difficult to access, and it took some time for the emergency services to reach the derailed carriages, several of which are believed to have been on fire. Sufficient medical staff are now in attendance, but there are still urgent pleas for further blood donors to come forward. Colleen Phillips, a London nurse who happened to be close to the location of the tragedy at the time and who offered her services to the rescue team, said that conditions were, and I quote, 'very difficult indeed'. Let's speak now to our reporter Simon Andrew, who's in a radio car about a mile from the site of the crash.*

★

JUST TERROR, WHAT else can you say? One minute you're asleep and the next there's the most almighty bang, and the whole train's in the air and being torn apart. I think it was the noise; you can't imagine what that sort of noise is like, and it comes out of nowhere.

It felt as though our carriage went down some kind of embankment; I thought it was going to turn over but it didn't, thank God. It was somehow up in the air, though, and there was a fire at the far end. Everything suddenly went dark and a woman was screaming and screaming; I think she must have been on fire. I can't forget that screaming; I don't think I ever will. Then I felt this guy hauling me up out of the seat and I somehow seemed to waken up. I suppose I was in total shock and just sitting there trying to make some kind of sense of the whole thing. He was saying to me he was going to get me out, that I was going to be all right, and he basically dragged me down onto the bank. I don't know where he went after that. I half lay there and it was as if all the sounds started coming through to me; it was like somebody turned up the volume. I had no idea where I was, but I suddenly felt freezing cold. And I don't suppose I was thinking straight; I realised I didn't have my jacket and that I should go back for it. And then all this wailing seemed to hit me; I could see a fire ahead of me and there was this terrible smell of burning. I thought of what must have happened and I just began crying; I remember calling out my husband's name, even though he hadn't been with me. The full shock of it just hit me and I felt terrified; it was a wave of fear that went through me, over and over. I don't know how long that went on for, and then this woman was holding me and just cradling me, rocking me. I suddenly looked at my hands and saw they were completely covered in blood. That was the first time

I became aware of any pain; before that I hadn't felt a thing. She just asked me what my name was and held me and rocked me, said my name over and over again as though I was a child. I still want to find the guy who must have saved my life. I realise I was incredibly fortunate; I imagine an awful lot of people must have been horrifically injured. All I think of still is that woman screaming, the one who must have been on fire. You can't get a sound like that out of your head. I don't know how you ever do.

★

'I WOULD LIKE first of all to express my outrage at the carnage inflicted on our nation in the early hours of this morning. We do know now that this was indeed a terrorist attack, and in choosing a train travelling from Edinburgh to London – from the north of our country to the very south – the terrorists were attacking representatives from every corner. There was a class of schoolchildren travelling to participate in a choir competition; there were ordinary men and women making journeys to visit relatives and travel home from holiday. It would be impossible to visit a site like this and not be moved by the evidence of such indiscriminate killing. But I'm also left angry – angry that this crime should be perpetrated in such a sickeningly heartless manner. Many people have been left with terrible burns; many more may die as a result of their injuries. We do not know precisely who has carried out such a cowardly attack but, make no mistake, we will turn over every single shred of evidence at this place of killing to ensure we do find the terrorists. I would ask all of you to be vigilant at this time and to inform the police of any suspicions you may have. Even the smallest piece of evidence may be important in tracking down those who committed this atrocity here at Burroway.

'I don't believe this is the time to stand on any kind of political platform. I am standing here this morning as a husband and a father, and my heart goes out to those who have lost their loved ones in a truly horrific manner. There must be a time for grieving first of all – that goes without saying – but then will come a time of root-and-branch searching for every clue that leads to the perpetrators of this hideous crime. And make no mistake, they will be hunted down, caught and punished – however long that may take. My thanks go to those of you from the media who have made the journey from London, and elsewhere, to be here at very short notice.'

★

'I WOULD LIKE to remind those assembled here today that this hearing is being held in complete secrecy, and that the anonymity of our witness is totally assured. He has volunteered to speak to the committee because of the information he possesses; it was his wish to make us aware of his evidence for the benefit of our inquiry. All we are at liberty to mention is that he is a senior officer with the Metropolitan Police, and that he has been in their ranks for over twenty years. So we would like to offer our sincere thanks to you for your willingness to address us today. We're extremely grateful.'

'Well, I realise the gravity of the situation and the responsibility that is placed upon us. I am also self-evidently aware of the vulnerability of my position and the need to speak cautiously, especially in light of recent revelations concerning the Met, and the unfortunate attention that has brought us. I think it's important to mention from the outset that my immediate superior – I am not even revealing his official rank to do all possible to protect his identity – lost his only brother in the Burroway bombing that morning. I would ask that this be kept in mind as I give my evidence, and may I assure the committee that I am providing as full an account as is possible.

'We did realise very quickly that this was a terrorist incident. I think that was officially revealed at about eleven o'clock in the morning, shortly before the statement the Prime Minister gave to the nation from the site of the bombing. But it was actually understood very early on: it was suspected from almost the first moment.

'Three of the four members of the terrorist group were killed outright by the blast; for some reason that we don't fully understand, the fourth member was farther back in the train at the time of the explosion. It may be that he actually lost his nerve at the last moment, or that he had perhaps started to doubt the validity of the whole operation long before. As I say, we simply don't know the answer to that at this point, but whatever the reason, the result was that he did manage to preserve his own life. In fact, it's not just a case of his surviving the explosion and the derailment and fire – he was actually all but unscathed. We were investigating the carriage where the bomb had been detonated and he basically staggered up to us. He was in a very distressed state and confessed his part in the atrocity from the outset. He was immediately put under arrest and taken to our car. It was still not fully light, and the whole episode was witnessed by no one else. Well, perhaps a more helpful way of expressing it is that there were few at the site of the bombing who would have paid attention to his presence or arrest at that moment. It has to be remembered that it was a scene of utter devastation: the living and the dead were being pulled from the remains of twisted carriages and life-saving treatment was being given to numerous individuals. From a police perspective, his appearance was almost too good to be true. Here was one surviving terrorist, completely unharmed, who could be removed from the scene without anyone observing a thing. From there he was taken to a secret location in London.'

★

*T*HE NUMBER OF *passengers who died when the sleeper from Edinburgh to King's Cross was blown up close to the hamlet of Burroway, some sixty miles north of London, has risen to a hundred and sixty-eight. Four of those who were seriously injured – an elderly man from Nottingham and three French students who were visiting the country as part of an exchange programme – have all died from the severe burns they suffered in one of the carriages that caught fire after the explosion on board. Police have now confirmed that all four of the suspects on the train were killed when the bomb they were carrying exploded at almost exactly four thirty this morning. The line is likely to remain closed for several days while every possible piece of evidence can be obtained, and as every attempt is made to establish the identities of a number of passengers who were caught in the worst of the firestorm that followed the explosion. Candlelit vigils will be held tonight in a number of cities, and many parish churches have already opened their doors to allow people to remember those who have died and those who have been left bereaved.*

There are growing calls for much more stringent controls on luggage at mainline stations, with some politicians saying that airport-style scanners must be brought in as swiftly as possible. The Home Secretary has said that while such measures will be considered again, it would be all but impossible to implement controls like these because of the sheer volume of passengers using the network on a daily basis. However, it seems likely that an inquiry will be set up to consider emergency measures in the light of the bombing and the risk of similar terrorist attacks.

★

I THINK BURROWAY was the last straw for Eric Semple. He believed we had been too liberal, that we were sleep-walking into catastrophe. He saw it in his own part of the north of England in particular, but that was essentially because he'd grown up there. It wasn't that he was blind to the situation elsewhere – in London, Birmingham and Manchester, as well as in other cities – it's that he had seen the effects of immigration on his home soil. I think the viciousness of the assault he'd suffered had an effect too. No charges were ever brought against those who'd most likely carried out the attack, and that stayed with him. The injustice of that. It was somehow symptomatic of the whole problem. Political correctness gone mad. You couldn't talk about this and you couldn't deal with that. If whites were guilty they were charged at once and the papers had a field day with the story. If the boot was on the other foot it was all nicely hushed up; it was better not to say anything at all. That enraged Eric. He had evidence of Sharia law being practised in the community and he took that to the police. Not a thing was done. A nice report was probably written and the whole thing shoved into a file that was pushed into a back drawer. Nothing made Eric more angry than that. I mean truly enraged. He could be frightening when he was like that, and at his most eloquent. The worst things always brought out the best in him, if that makes any sense. The best time to get Eric to make a political speech and really rouse people was when he was furious, when the fire inside him had been lit. He was a man who truly believed in his own politics, not like the vast majority of career politicians today who've learned their manifestos and their party scripts. He had no time for that either, whether they were on the left or the right or stuck in the centre.

He believed passionately that there was a section of Islam that wanted to take this country over. That lay at the heart of Eric. The conviction that that was their ultimate goal and that we were letting them get there, step by tiny step. He felt certain there was some kind of secret movement that had that at the top of its agenda. I don't think he had any proof; I suspect he didn't have a shred of actual proof. But he would have said that was partly because we were so bloody obsessed with political correctness! We were too frightened to turn over the stones that needed to be turned over. We were so busy pussy-footing around the Muslim community, bending over backwards to sort out their grievances and build them schools and mosques and the rest of it, that we turned a totally blind eye to what was crying out to be investigated. He felt very sorry for the police in particular because he felt their hands were tied more and more tightly politically. Of course he blamed his local force for having two left feet and being inefficient, but he was well aware of the politics too. How do you arrest a black man with a gun when he immediately accuses you of racist treatment? Eric Semple just thought we had lost the plot and thrown away the script. That was why he stood for election in the Sudburgh constituency however many weeks after the Burroway bombing. He was still full of rage against those young idiots who had destroyed so many lives. He wanted to make a difference, to wake people up.

I think he thought twice about it. His daughter was at an important stage in secondary school and he was concerned for her and concerned for his wife. He and Trish were very close. He was a good father and husband, whatever rubbish the press come out with now. They know nothing: they'll use whatever ammunition they can find and chuck in anything else that comes to hand. I know that the only doubt Eric Semple had over standing for election was in regard to the effect that it might have on his family.

Of course he stood as an independent: what else would he have done? He would never have been so stupid as to stand on a White Rose platform. That would have been madness. No, I'm not about to say whether or not he was a member of White Rose at that time or before it – I simply refuse. All I can say is that of course he stood as an independent: it was the *best* thing to do and in fact it was the *only* thing to do.

★

I THINK I was radicalised, whatever that really means. I think there are different degrees, obviously, and I know people who were far more extreme than I was ever likely to become. I was at university in Manchester, studying science. I'm from a mixed background: my father's parents came over from Pakistan, but my mum's from North Wales. I suspect school was probably toughest: I was at a rough comprehensive, which had better remain nameless, and I got bullied like hell. I was good at sport and everything, but I was just a mess racially! I don't think I had a clue who I really was. We drove up to North Wales for the summer holidays and my mother's cousins were all chattering in Welsh. You want to be part of a world; you want to fit in and be accepted, and some of the time I suppose I felt that. I learned a few words of the language and that helped a bit, but it wasn't enough. It could never be enough. I was just left feeling frustrated. Then I went with my Dad to Pakistan when I was probably seventeen; I knew bits and pieces of Urdu, really from my grandparents, but it wasn't enough. So on both sides I had this really huge sense of inadequacy, that I really didn't fit in anywhere and probably never would.

It was worthwhile in one respect because it meant I worked incredibly hard over the last two years of secondary, when it really counted. I did that pretty much by myself; I can't remember one teacher at school who pushed or encouraged me. I think the whole lot of them were too knackered. Most of the time what they were doing was crowd control. There was at least one fight every day. Fights were actually planned ahead of time; it was probably the most exciting thing that happened. I suppose if you've been facing that year after year, with classes of kids who don't want to be there and don't want to learn, you give up trying in the end.

I'm not sure the staff even realised I was working; I'm not even certain it would have bothered them to know. There were perhaps one or two who would have cared, but it wasn't something I was about to show either. You kept your head down, pretended the whole thing was boring. If it looked as though you were working hard, your life would have been a nightmare. But I think

I started to push myself because of that inner identity crisis. I didn't know who I was and I almost wanted to stop thinking about it, going over it and over it in my head. This was a kind of burying your head in the sand. In a strange way I wasn't thinking; I was filling myself with scientific facts, and maybe that felt good because everything else around me was blurred.

I don't think I talked to my parents about it at all. I'm not sure I would have known where to start; I don't think I'd have had the right language. My mother was working and out till all hours; I only learned midway through university that she was also having an affair. But I did know that she and Dad didn't get on well, hadn't really for many years. That was another reason to hide in the house, to live behind a closed door.

Anyway, I got myself to university – the first from my family. I'm not sure any of the rest of them would have known how to spell university. What I found from the beginning were friends, the first real friends I'd had in my life. And it so happened they were Islamic; they were really excited about religion and about politics. Yeah, I did vaguely know three of those who went on to commit the Burroway bombing – I was aware of the guys. I'm not even certain I ever spoke to any of them, but I did know who they were. They tended to go round as a group; they were their own inner circle, if you like. I'm not sure how the girl fitted in; it may have been she joined them later. But yes, I suppose you can say I was on the edge of the same set. I still don't feel I truly belonged; I was always conscious of half belonging and half not. But the paradox is that that may have made me all the more committed. I desperately wanted to have an identity in my life; I was longing to be accepted. I was excited by the fact I had real friends for the first time. I wanted to learn their language in every sense. And the irony is that during my first year I hardly attended lectures; I had slaved away to get to university, but now that I had got there, I had somehow found something better, more valuable. One girl in the group even started teaching me Urdu; I can remember we did hours in the library. I hardly went home at all in that first year; I was far happier meeting up with the group at weekends, just spending hours talking and arguing. Not all of it was political by any means, but a lot of it was. A lot of it was about being a Muslim in Britain and what that meant, what it was going to mean in the future. About the rise of the right and in particular White Rose, to what lengths we should fight against it. How far we should go. Effectively what was right and what was too far. We were living in our own world. I think we were almost unaware of what was going on outside, if you like. It was dangerous in so much as it was a virtual reality. I suppose that can be true whatever set of people you swirl around you. I think I came to believe some pretty frightening things. I think I would have done some pretty scary things. If you're fired up by four hours of talk and it's two in the morning and you're twenty-one, you're willing to go out and do pretty much anything. But I'll tell you what I honestly believe:

I reckon it's always been that way. I think it's been that way since the beginning of time.

★

I NEVER SAW the Prime Minister as disturbed as he was in the days immediately following the Burroway bombing. I had been his Private Secretary for two years by then, and we had been through some pretty tough waters. We all know the role becomes tougher almost with each new election: the pressure from journalists, the scrutiny of select committees, the demands of lobby groups. We know our leaders are mortal and it seems that almost the moment we elect them we blame them for being so.

But the bombing brought him to his knees. He was quite shattered by the implications. It came from nowhere and left him reeling. He cared deeply about community relations and had good friends in the Islamic world. He almost took it as a personal insult. I think that for several days he simply didn't know what to do and blamed himself for that. It was a vicious circle and he couldn't escape.

He talked to me quite openly about his confusion and depression. Our relationship had always been warm and with room for a good degree of humour, but never before had he confided in me to such a degree. He simply wanted to talk, to talk the whole thing out. To begin with I didn't feel confident enough to offer answers, but he almost brushed that to one side. It was as though he considered it irrelevant. It was clear he felt his vulnerability as never before, and there was no one else to whom he could reveal such vulnerability. I mean, no one else in his political circle; I'm not talking about those outwith that circle.

Perhaps it made a difference that I was a woman, that he knew I was a listener – and that he could confide in me, obviously. I think certainly he was aware I wasn't judgemental, that I wasn't about to be shocked at his apparent weakness. I think I was glad he chose to confide in me as he did. I don't simply mean honoured in some petty, vainglorious way, I mean I did care about his personal well-being; I had learned to respect the man he was – beyond the politician – and it meant something to talk on that level.

Not that I remember offering solutions, and not that I think he sought them from me, It was somehow as though he was unfolding a map on the floor, bit by bit; that's the best analogy I can find. He was trying to fold out all the corners, to get a sense of the lie of the land.

I don't think it was the opposition that frightened him. Yes, of course, he had to face the baying and the baiting at the weekly ordeal of Prime Minister's Question Time, but he had somehow got used to that by then.

He was a quick thinker and a good orator, and he knew it. No, what I think he feared far more was quite simply what was going to happen next. He had been genuinely moved visiting the scene of the bombing; he had found it very difficult to stand in the middle of it all and speak to camera. But if this could happen out of the blue, with no warning whatsoever, then what on earth was next? It was that sheer sense of powerlessness to control the forces that now seemed to have been unleashed, and set against him. He took it very personally, and I cannot say I blame him. Who wouldn't have? It was all about putting the genie back in the bottle, and how on earth do you do that?

★

'THIS MORNING WE'RE joined by the leader of White Rose, Andrew Gregory, and I'm going to begin, Mr Gregory, by rather boldly asking you about your own role in that position. You're certainly not the kind of leader we might imagine: you're very much what we would describe as middle class, you're university educated and you're well spoken…'

'But I think all that you're listing actually says far more about you than it does about me! You've created some kind of preconceived idea as to what the leader of this sort of organisation should be, and that's patent nonsense. It's as stupid – and pointless – as my having an idea of you as a beer-swilling, chain-smoking journalist who does only liquid lunches! I think you know as well as I do that we have to get away from stereotypes in this world, that stereotypes are far more unhelpful than helpful in the long run.'

'All right, point taken, but can we all the same think about the average member of White Rosé? Would you not admit that most of our viewers will have some kind of idea, rightly or wrongly, of the standard White Rose supporter?'

'No, I will certainly admit that! I am well aware that many of our members – though not all of them by any means – are white working-class men. But I believe that says a great deal about our political system and the way in which a great swathe of our society has been neglected over the past decades. The Labour Party simply ceased to be for working people. All the major political parties focused their primary attention on the middle-class vote, and they simply disregarded an underclass that in their opinion wasn't worth bothering about because most of its members didn't vote! So if I think of White Rose as anything, I think of it as a political party. It's unashamedly for the white people of this island who have been neglected and even discriminated against for the past decades.'

'Would you say that you hate immigrants?'

'No, I do not hate immigrants. I do have a huge problem with those who come here and who want to import their belief systems and their laws and who, in the end, actually want to take over our country. I have a huge problem with those who seek to achieve that by planting bombs and creating carnage among innocent, law-abiding citizens of this country, which has been generous enough to adopt them. I believe strongly that there are people who shouldn't be allowed to come here to begin with, and I believe equally strongly that there are people who should be deported. And in both cases, it should not be nearly so difficult to achieve those ends. I think those are entirely reasonable aspirations.'

'So will White Rose become a political party?'

'Well, that's not for me to decide, but I actually believe it's better that we remain political with a small p. There are certainly no formal plans to have candidates standing for election, either at local or national level, and I would definitely prefer that that remains the case. The fact of the matter is that we are campaigning on one major issue. Party political candidates are there to cover a multitude of issues; they are dealing with everything from new roads to nuclear weapons. I think you see something of the difficulty of that transition from protest organisation to political party in the operations of the Scottish National Party. In the 1970s they were much more of a romantic movement than any kind of fully fledged party. They were about one major issue. The difficulty came, paradoxically enough, when they were swept into office after growing exponentially. They then had to become men – and women – in grey suits, and it became harder and harder to deal with the very issue that had brought them to power in the first place!'

'I want to ask you about an issue that has drawn a lot of attention to you since you came into being, and that's the burka. You think it should be illegal, don't you?'

'Yes, I do. No ifs and no buts; I believe it should be banned. When I see the veil rendering a woman's face to nothing more than a pillar-box slit, I actually find myself wanting to rip it off. As far as I'm concerned, this is taking us back to the medieval period, and it should have no place in our Western society. I realise that's controversial, but I'm glad that I'm part of an organisation that stands for controversial things. I see around me party leaders who are bending over backwards to conform, refusing to step out of line, desperately trying to please everyone. I think the fact that membership of White Rose has grown at times by over 20,000 a month says something about just how fed up the people of our island are with conformity and with political correctness. I hope I live to see the day when the burka is illegal in Britain, and when the women who have worn it are no longer treated like chattels. But I'm honest enough to admit that that day is still far off on the horizon. An awful lot of fighting will have to be done first.'

★

'So may I ask what then happened to your prisoner once he was brought to London?'

'Yes, as I've mentioned, he was taken to a secret location that I would ask not to be revealed even now. We made contact with certain individuals on our way, and during the journey – perhaps even as a result of that contact – he was often extremely agitated. That having been said, as soon as we got to London he seemed to calm down a good deal. We were aware, self-evidently, that even though he had just confessed to his part in the bomb attack, he had been through the horror of it all himself. He was given a full medical examination, he was permitted to rest for a time, and he was given a full change of clothing. His own clothing was in a terrible state and he had blood and grime on his hands. I omitted to mention that he was able to shower before changing.

'He was then taken to a normal interview room for questioning and brought a light meal since he claimed he had eaten nothing whatsoever since leaving Edinburgh. And by the time that had all happened it was perhaps two o'clock in the afternoon. There were two of us present to question him, and I can remember almost at once feeling I was with a totally different person.'

'I'm not quite sure I follow. What exactly do you mean?'

'That he had calmed down entirely. He was relaxed, almost confident, and all the gibbering nonsense we had heard in the car was gone. I would say he was almost arrogant the way he sat there; the fear had certainly gone entirely, and I felt the whole business of questioning him was pretty much pointless.'

'How long were you there for? And what about your superior? Was he present throughout this time too?'

'I'm sorry, I should have made it clear that he had left almost as soon as we arrived at the place. I didn't know why, but he was gone for at least a couple of hours. He would have returned at about four o'clock, and it was then I learned of his brother. I left the interview room and found him outside, ashen-faced. He told me that his only brother had been on the sleeper, that his body had been recovered. I didn't know what to say; I found the whole situation very awkward. We had never operated on anything but a formal level; I wouldn't say that it was a cold relationship, but it was most certainly strictly formal. I have no idea what I said, though I obviously made some kind of attempt to show my sympathy. He just stayed where he was for a long time – perhaps twenty minutes or longer. He sat facing the wall, not moving, and I remember thinking I had never seen anyone so pale in all my life. Then he just got up, put down the empty mug of tea he had drunk, and looked straight at me. His face might have been made of stone. It was devoid of emotion.

'"What do you want me to do, sir?" I asked.

'"Squeeze him till he squeals," he answered.'

★

'WE HAVE BEEN prepared to be second-class citizens too long. I go to London and I sit on the upper deck of a bus, and I wonder where I am. But it isn't just London: it's Sudburgh too. I heard of a white English woman who learned Urdu in the end because she was so lonely in her neighbourhood and no one spoke to her. I'm going to see to it that a few more people learn English if I'm elected in this constituency.

'It might come as a surprise to you to hear that I'm sad the four who committed the Burroway bombing all died. I'll tell you why I feel sad. Because it was too easy a death. Were I to have had my way, all four of them would have faced the death penalty. Think of the people affected by that tragedy. But what would have happened to the perpetrators had they survived? At worst they would have faced life sentences. With you, me and everyone in this hall paying however many hundred thousand a year to keep them behind bars every year. What sort of lunacy is that? What sort of comfort would it be to those who lost parents and children and beloved friends on that train? I think to myself what they might have faced back in Pakistan. If they were lucky enough to make it to prison it would hardly be the bed of roses that incarceration is in England.

'But it's not just about flogging and hanging. I can see the tabloids tomorrow morning: Eric Semple wants to bring back the death penalty. Oh no, ladies and gentlemen, it's about a whole lot more than that. Eric Semple wants to restore sanity. He wants to make being

English and white normal again, instead of something that's been reduced to something of an embarrassment. My grandfather fought for this country and he loved it; I can remember that even into his eighties when the National Anthem was played on Christmas Day after the Queen's Speech he swayed onto his rickety legs because he was proud. There was no one would take his pride from him. He didn't boast about what he'd done in the war; he didn't even talk about it, no more than most of the men who fought. He just came back home to be English and British and live in the country he'd fought for.

'You know what I sometimes think of this country as it is now? As a car park for refugees and economic migrants. And we can't accommodate them. We go on ushering in hundreds of thousands more each year and we can't even house our own teenagers. Now I realise that you voting for me is not going to change the whole country; it's not going to mean blue sky and sunlight for the rest of your lives. But what I can promise is that I will work with blood, sweat and tears for the rights of those people I feel have been marginalised far too long. And I will work to see that this constituency isn't just an anomaly, but that like-minded spirits have the courage to stand up for the kind of values I've been praising tonight. I would like to see pride restored in this city of ours, and I believe it can be done. But I think it has to be done by someone who takes immigration and race relations seriously, who deals with what has to be dealt with and doesn't just come out with the usual party statements. This has all been put to one side for far too long, ladies and gentlemen, and I intend to do something about that, at a national as well as a local level. So I ask for your vote and I ask for your confidence: I am a man of my word and I am a fighter. I look forward to fighting for you.'

★

*I*T HAS BEEN *announced by Downing Street that a garden of remembrance is to be created at the site of the Burroway bombing. A number of high-profile artists have been invited to create works that will be displayed there, and the sonnet that the Poet Laureate published shortly after the tragedy will be inscribed in the final slab of a stone pathway together with the names of all those who perished. Downing Street will not confirm that the idea for the memorial garden came from the Prime Minister himself, and he has stated that the question itself is a distraction, that remembering those who died in the tragedy should be the business of all those interested in strengthening tolerance and democracy. Nevertheless, it is believed that he was very much behind the original idea for the creation of a permanent memorial to the victims.*

The intention is to design the garden in such a way

that it can be seen from the train, something that will be important to the many who are not able to visit the site on foot due to its relative inaccessibility. A number of well-known Asian artists have been invited to offer their work for possible inclusion, despite vociferous protests from White Rose. It has not been revealed who will be part of the final line-up of artists, and part of the reason for this is believed to be that at least one Asian artist will be included.

The organisation behind the creation of the garden has said it is hugely important to remember that at least thirty people from the Asian community were among those who died in the bombing, and that no single group or community should be seen to have ownership of the Burroway memorial. The Prime Minister was not available for comment earlier today, but Downing Street did confirm that he would make a formal announcement concerning the garden in the coming days. Money for the creation of the memorial will come primarily from one anonymous source; various other organisations in England and Scotland have committed parcels of funding. The Palace has expressed full commitment to the work, and it is fully expected that a member of the Royal Family will officially open the memorial once it is complete.

★

I REMEMBER SEEING a change in those in my school after the bombing. I am thirteen and back then I was just ten. There was a lot of name-calling; sometimes the bigger boys threw stones at us across the street. We weren't included in games in the same way: I can remember someone shouting that if the ball was kicked to us it might blow up. Everyone laughed even though it wasn't very clever.

I came home from school once and felt very upset; I'm not sure what it was that had got me so down – I think just the long drip-drip effect of it all. I hugged my mother and felt the tears hot at the back of my eyes; I asked her why it was everyone hated us. She looked at me with such sadness; she bent down to my level and her hands were white with the flour she had been using for baking. She smiled at me, but it was more a kind of crying. She showed me her hands then and she said that whatever we did we would never be white. We had been made the way we were and there was no reason to be ashamed. She said that God loved the heart of people, that He did not care about the outer skin. She said that human beings were the ones who were worried about what colour we were, but that God was interested in who we were inside.

I nodded and I understood that she was right, but I still felt so full of sadness. I don't think I had ever felt such sadness before in all my life. My mother saw that and understood without saying anything. She left the baking and washed the flour from her hands and she carried me upstairs. I was far too old to be carried but I felt comforted when she did that. She sat me down at the window ledge in my room and she sat behind me and held me. She rocked me gently from side to side and she sang me a song I could remember from when I was a baby. I could not remember all of it, but somehow it was there in me all the same. It was a song that had come down through her family and was very precious to her. I could tell she was crying as she sang it and rocked me, but I never looked round once.

★

I THINK THE Prime Minister really did reach some kind of crisis point at that time. I've never said so openly before, but I think I can after all these years. It would have felt like disloyalty at an earlier time, but I do think that this sort of party solidarity can become quite ridiculous at times. Never admitting there's been a disappointment, always insisting on talking in upbeat terms. I'm well aware that the electorate, at least what one might call the wise core of the electorate, are simply not fooled. If you lose a bloody by-election then have the honesty to say it was a disappointment! I remember once listening back to one of these dreadful radio interviews with politicians after a by-election – I can't for the life of me remember which one it was and it doesn't really matter now – and from the sound of it you would have thought no one had lost at all!

At any rate, that's all part of a wider question. I suspect that being somewhat longer in the tooth helps, and being a good deal further out of the eye of the storm. The less you have to lose the more you feel you can say. I think the best example of that was seen in Tony Benn. He became a maverick: he said precisely what he wanted to say and did so most eloquently. But the only time he certainly didn't was when he was right at the heart of government! Perhaps I say all this to comfort myself; all of us are guilty of it.

Yes, I think back to the time immediately following Burroway. There was something of a firestorm in White-hall that this couldn't have come more out of the blue. These four hadn't been watched for a moment: they were on no one's radar. I think the Prime Minister barely slept in the days following the whole thing; he did a tremen-dous amount, but he actually ended up attempting to do too much. He was in effect trying to be both Prime Minister and Head of State. I've never quite understood why he took the whole think so personally: perhaps it was quite simply because he felt he had built up such good relations with the Asian community, that he had established a genuine trust with leaders up and down the country. But it felt like something more and I have no way of knowing if I'm right or not. All of it will come out one day, decades after most of us are dead.

What I can speak about now is his marriage. That had been under quite immense pressure during the preceding months, and I think there was still a sense in the party, and perhaps even in the country, that a strong marriage at the heart of government was something of a sine qua non. So there was all the strain of trying to keep things together and not give away anything of the real struggle behind the scenes. Oh, she wanted a divorce – a separation at the very least – and she didn't care one whit what damage that did to him. Perhaps she even wanted to inflict that damage and would have been quite happy for it to happen then.

I think all of us in the Cabinet felt desperately sorry for him, but in point of fact there was very little we could have done. I think it's when the political world is at its very loneliest; you have spent all these years working your way up not just one but several greasy poles, and you feel you are going to slide all the way down if you suddenly show weakness. I simply don't think it's an option if you're PM. And I'm not honestly sure he had any truly close friends in the House; that's sad to admit, but I think it would be true. So it must have been an incredibly lonely time for him.

I think the whole Eric Semple thing rather gave him breathing space, paradoxically enough. Of course to a large degree they were linked – one almost flowed into the other – but the actual white-hot focus on Burroway lessened. Once the memorial garden was under construction I think the PM actually began to relax somewhat, to let his shoulders drop just a little. That garden meant a very great deal to him personally; I know there have been cynical suggestions it was about little more than keeping people quiet, but that's actually most unjust. He wanted there to be some kind of provision for people's grief – not least his own! – and he wanted the place to be visible from passing trains. And let's remember that despite its quite ludicrously inaccessible position, thousands upon thousands did go to pay their respects in the weeks and months that followed. I think all that did something to rebuild him personally, to allow him to feel he had somehow done the right thing. It's as though he felt the bombing was his personal fault: it had been carried out on his watch. The creation of a garden of remembrance was not about winning any kind of glory; it was about having perhaps done the right thing – neither more nor less than that. And I feel he did believe in the end he had done that.

★

THE DREAM? Do you not know about the dream? That must have been about three or four days before the by-election. I suppose Trish would have told me about it afterwards, a long time later. It really annoys me now what they write about Eric and Trish: I suppose it's true that what some newspapers don't know they'll simply make up. Trish and I were always good friends, but we didn't see a tremendous amount of each other – we both had busy family lives. It was really only later, after everything had happened, that we drew much closer, and that was good.

Well, it's quite simple really – Trish had some fearful nightmare and woke up screaming. That may sound faintly ridiculous. What on earth would be seen as out of the ordinary about that? Don't we all have at least one such nightmare in our lives for whatever reason? And wasn't it the case that she was under a great deal of stress anyway because of the by-election and everything that might lie ahead? All of that is true, but Trish had had some very vivid dream about Eric; she hadn't actually seen what happened to him in the end, but she had been aware of some strange underground place and vivid faces. She said to me it was like a film; she felt she was there, somewhere in the shadows, watching and listening. She knew without any shadow of doubt it had to do with Eric, that something terrible was happening to Eric – and *would* happen to Eric.

At any rate she woke up screaming and she and Eric got up in the middle of the night and went downstairs. Didn't matter what Eric was doing in the morning, all that he still had to finish in the last hours of campaigning – that's the kind of guy he was, and I wish the papers knew it. All this had been almost thrust upon him anyway; five years before he'd never have believed he'd be standing as a candidate in a by-election. So Trish told him the whole thing and he sat and listened; she basically begged him to let the whole thing go, not to go ahead with it. She believed that what she'd dreamed had something to do with his election, that there was no earthly doubt the two were inextricably linked.

The polls were still putting the Tories ahead, though it's true that Eric looked like coming strongly in second place. But Eric had no real sense then of the idea of winning; he was an independent candidate with no political history who was making race relations his core message. He was pleased to be giving speeches on what he cared about passionately, but there was almost a naivety about him regarding being elected. That was the strange thing: he was a very complicated figure, hard to get the full measure of. You could hear Eric making a speech and when the wind was in his sails it could be quite frightening; someone once called him a little Hitler, and the nickname stuck, though it made him very uncomfortable. It was a very dubious compliment. But he was certainly a force to be reckoned with on nights like that, and he was often at his best when he wasn't reading or half reading from a script. When he really was in full flight he was at his best, and he knew it; the words seemed to come from nowhere. It was actually like a kind of flying.

And then you saw him at home, when he'd just been with young kids. He adored babies: you could sit Eric

with a baby and he'd be lost for hours. Soft as butter, a
gentle sense of fun – kindness itself. He related superbly
well to men; he got to know them in a real way, could
get right under their skin. I think he liked women too,
and he most certainly adored Trish, but it was getting
alongside men he was best at. He was powerfully built
and there was an edge to his voice, so working men
especially respected him, but he could be kind and a
good listener if he needed to be. Just as I said he was the
night of Trish's nightmare. But it went way beyond his
own family: he listened to people within the community.
Working men who simply felt discriminated against,
who felt second-class citizens within their own country.
He just knew how to get alongside them. There was more
than one Eric Semple. Of course, it's true of all of us; that
goes without saying. But it's just important to remember
there were many Eric Semples. I think it matters a lot to
remember it.

So that was the way it was that night with Trish. He
went downstairs with her and would have sat with her
for an hour or more while she told him her dream and
begged him to give the whole thing up. Maybe he did
consider it for a minute; I don't know. But the truth was
that he simply didn't believe it was an issue, that he was
going to win. He knew what the big old parties were like,
they rallied their troops and won through in the end. He
didn't really believe he was going to break through all
that history. He wanted to make people think. I reckon at
that point, in the middle of the night seventy-two hours

or whatever before the actual vote, what mattered to him more than anything was that people started thinking. He always felt that people didn't think enough: they voted the way their parents had voted and that somehow felt safest. Nothing drove him madder than that. He wanted to waken people up and make people angry; he almost felt that was his task, his mission. But he didn't truly believe he was ever going to win that by-election.

And that was what he said to Trish. That there was no need to give up because he wasn't going to win; it simply wasn't about to happen. And there was nothing she could say to make him change his mind.

★

I THINK IF anything we were a bit too nice to him. I feel almost embarrassed saying that now, because I've dealt with the toughest and had them in tears. And felt no shame about it, I can tell you. If you're interrogating a man you know has beaten up his wife for decades, or someone who's almost certainly been molesting a child, perhaps also for years, you learn to turn on a cold tap. That's what my best instructor told me when it came to interrogation: learn to turn on a cold tap. The best criminals could have degrees in psychology; the best prison inmates certainly could! They might not be able to explain what they're able to do in terms of manipulation, but they'll achieve it again and again.

Yes, I apologise for digressing. I think it's important to state that we were soft on him all the same: it was just so apparent that he was a boy who hadn't quite grown up yet. I had to keep reminding myself that he had been involved – no, at the very heart of – a terrorist attack of quite unimaginable proportions, and that he and his fellow terrorists had turned the country upside-down. He had been responsible, along with three others, for creating a near crisis at the heart of government. But for all that, I think I didn't see him as a threat: he did not come across as any great convert to extreme Islamic ideology who oozed some dark malevolence. What he talked about was verging on the petty: the long talks at university, the watching of certain films. I felt quite certain that he was the wrong man in that he was not the ringleader. He seemed much more the spare wheel on the wagon; now he was polite and wanting to answer the questions we asked to the best of his ability. I failed to believe that this was double bluff; in all conscience, he didn't seem bright enough for that. I felt after two hours that it was purely and simply a case of the wrong man having survived: this guy had been the hanger-on and in the end the coward, and attempting to wring something out of him that simply wasn't there was next to pointless.

Then my superior – the officer I've talked about from the outset – came back at about seven o'clock. I can remember thinking that there was a strangeness about his face. He was pale and drawn and there was something strange about his expression. I have said that I didn't know him well and that our relationship was strictly professional: if truth be told, I had never got the impression that he liked me much. I had thought that on several occasions before, but it was almost an irrelevance: it was simply of no consequence what he thought of me. We worked alongside each other from time to time; it was neither less nor more than that. I think what muddied the waters now was my knowledge of his loss: that his only brother had been killed in the Burroway bombing. I was very aware of that, especially at the moment when I saw his expression and tried to read it. But nor could I be certain that what I was reading was correct.

At any rate, I noticed that he was carrying a small satchel with him when he came into the interview room. He asked if he could speak with me and I got up at once, went outside and closed the door behind me. He wouldn't look at me and his eyes seemed everywhere; he was impatient and very clipped. He didn't actually let on that he was frustrated we had got so little from our prisoner, detainee – call him what you will – but that was abundantly clear all the same. He seemed to brush aside all that I mumbled about his not seeming to have much to reveal, nor a great deal of malice in him. I realised how it must have come across, but I genuinely believed now that we were in danger of flogging something of a dead horse.

He interrupted me in the end and spoke quickly and without looking at me; that is what I will always remember, that he almost *refused* to look at me. That is the verb I would use. He said that down below this floor of the building there was a chamber that had been used in the old days for interrogations – that was the word he used more than once – and that was where he wanted to take him now. This was about the defence of the realm; it was of the utmost importance that we got from him every shred of evidence that might be used to prevent a similar or even a far more serious atrocity. Did I not realise that he might be quite capable of letting us believe he was really the innocent in the whole affair? That was something he had encountered time and again in Northern Ireland; you released the rat into the streets again and two months later the rat came back with Semtex and blew a few lives to smithereens. We had a chance to find out the whole truth; we had one survivor and it was our duty, our moral responsibility, to get the last drop of evidence from him, however long that took. And he said that he would do the interrogating, that that was what he wanted, insisted on.

I felt there was little more I could say or do at that point. I followed him back to the interview room and was asked at no time whether I agreed with what was being suggested or not. In point of fact it would be wrong to say it was being suggested: it was more a case of the whole thing being demanded. It had been decided; there seemed no room for discussion. How did I feel? I will admit that I felt I had been rather driven over. It was only later, I suppose, I felt aggrieved about it and even something verging on anger or at least great frustration. I felt brushed to one side; the manner in which we had conducted things was just dismissed. Interestingly enough, I remember seeing my superior by the prisoner for a second in the interview room and recalling something. It came back to me that once upon a time, many years before, there had been allegations, rumours – never substantiated – that he had punched a black suspect. I can remember nothing else about the case than that; all of the circumstances have gone now, but that simply flashed across my mind, the memory of that allegation. Then he explained very quickly and not very clearly what was going to happen next and we all meekly followed him out of the interview room.

No, I had no real idea what this was all about – none. It sounds an excuse to say everything happened terribly quickly, but it is nothing less than the truth. He had suddenly come back to the building, had dragged me out and swept to one side all I tried to explain, offered his own solution and decided he was going to be the one to do the interrogating from then on. Yes, I know that he was perfectly within his rights, but I believe – and continue to believe – that what he was deciding was simply not up to him alone. I don't feel I actually thought there was anything malevolent about his actions at that point: I felt more that I had been caught up in a whirlwind and deprived of time to think and make decisions.

I felt that on behalf of my colleague, too. There were two of us who had been conducting the interview, the questioning – and we were equally dismissed. I'm not sure whether we actually spoke about the whole thing together later or not; we were both too shell-shocked. So we basically proceeded into this back place – this old Victorian rooms and stairs – and started down into a kind of basement. But if the two of us felt bewildered, I can hardly imagine what was going through the mind of our prisoner. He was just beside himself with terror.

★

No, it wasn't hearing about the bombing itself that came first. It just so happened that I went downstairs very early in the morning and put on the radio. There are times I think when you feel something catastrophic has taken place, and this was one of them. It had nothing to do with second sight at that moment, nothing at all. It was just the kind of feeling I suspect we all have now and again in our lives when we know something has happened. I just sat numb with a cup of tea by the window; the radio was hardly on at all because I was afraid I might waken my husband upstairs. In the end I ceased to hear the individual words that were spoken at all: my eyes were on the beauty of the early-morning sky and they filled with tears.

I couldn't tell you when I saw the vision, if that's what I'm to call it; I never really know how to describe such things. I'm from the north-west Highlands of Scotland and I have the second sight, have had it since I was a young child. I don't believe you choose to have such a thing: indeed, if most people could choose whether they'd have it or not I suspect they would wish it away in a moment.

It's very hard to describe how it works with me. Quite suddenly I'll be taken outside myself altogether: it's almost as though a door into another world opens and I'm inside for a few seconds. Except that you have no sense whatsoever of the passage of time; I have no real way of knowing whether it all lasts five seconds or five minutes. Most often it happens when I'm on my own, and it seems to be when I'm quite far away in my thoughts anyway. So you're slipping from a place of – I simply don't know how to express it properly. In Scotland we talk about being in a dwam; the way you might be on a bus when you're looking into the landscape and are far away in your thoughts. It's not necessarily a place of deep thinking; you may not be consciously thinking of anything at all. It's somehow beyond that.

At any rate, I had this flash of a vision of a river of blood. It was in a town or a city, and I knew it was a place where I had never been before. I cannot tell you how I knew that, I can say only that I *did* know it, pure and simple. Although it lasted for only a moment, for that split second I could see with absolute clarity the buildings on either side of the road and even the shapes of the clouds in the sky. It was as clear as any photograph, but it all happened so quickly – rather like a flash of lightning – so you are left with only the detail of this single picture you've been given.

But I did know with certainty, right away, it was a river of blood. I could tell it was flowing, don't ask me how. There was just no doubt about that part of it, and I really knew at once that this was linked to the bombing. I don't believe it represented the bombing itself; I knew it was somehow connected to it. The fact was that this was somewhere different; I just knew it. It *felt* a different place too. I realise that a lot of my explanation is going to make little or no sense, especially to anyone who takes a healthy amount of convincing about things. I can say only that this is the best way I can describe what I suffer; it is the most honest way. I really didn't sleep that night; I was wondering if there was anything I could do to work out where this place might be, to prevent some terrible catastrophe before it was too late. It didn't strike me at the time that the vision might have been a metaphor; most of what I'm shown is literal. But all I could do was remember the sight of that flowing blood; I felt I could all but smell it. And why was this given to me? I don't think I'll ever know; I often don't. I just suffer with something until it makes a kind of sense. But in the end I felt there was nothing I could do with it, except remember it and see that blood and smell it. I think it was a warning, nothing less than a warning of what was to come.

★

GEORGE CARR, CONSERVATIVE *Party – nine thousand, two hundred and twenty-four. Marjory Karen Ellis, Labour Party – six thousand, one hundred and ten. Laurence Kelly, Liberal Democrat – one thousand, nine hundred and seventy-six. Francis Eric Semple – nine thousand, seven hundred and twelve. I hereby declare that Francis Eric Semple...*

The place just erupted after that. I think Eric was the most surprised of the lot. I remember his face being quite ashen; he blinked a lot and was holding Trish's hand, but he hardly seemed to notice what was going on around him. It was like a football stadium. With his name being roared so much he was barely able to speak, and he didn't say much in the end. The Tories had really believed they'd won it; I think he believed it himself, right up to the nail. I'm not sure his own supporters did, though; they were jubilant, but they'd fought and fought for every vote. And that was what did it: five hundred votes was the difference between success and failure in the end.

I noticed Eric was whisked away quite quickly. There was a struggle to get him out of a side door; it looked as if things were going to get a bit ugly at one point. He had his heavyweight champions: a couple of Neanderthals who could have broken their way through concrete. There were English flags flying, some far-right inflammatory chanting. The media were going wild; there were television crews – not only from this country – and all manner of interviews taking place. Everyone knew what Eric stood for: he was an independent in name only. This was a first, a total first. It was one thing being voted onto a local council, but winning a seat in a by-election was something else.

The spin being put on it already was that it was the Burroway effect, that Eric had stood on a xenophobic, anti-Islamic platform and tapped into far-right sympathies. I suppose that wasn't all wrong either; he certainly benefitted from the Burroway tragedy – perhaps he wouldn't have won at all without it. But what was more true was that the whole mood of the country was quite anti-Islamic: people were really angry at the carnage, at the slaughter of total innocents. Eric had been bold in his speech-making: he wasn't called Little Hitler for nothing. Quite what they thought he could do to change the position is another matter; it was almost that they could just feel a bit better about the state of the world and their lives if he was elected – that was as important as anything else.

People spilled out onto the streets after that and it

65

was a warm and muggy night. There was a party atmosphere and you could hear chanting and clapping all around. One or two pubs were serving free drinks and I remember hearing fireworks going off. I'm not sure what I thought, to be honest. I was quite excited that he'd done it, that he'd proved all the pundits wrong. But I can also remember thinking I was glad I didn't come from the Pakistani community. I can't say I thought about that for any length of time, but I certainly can remember it being something that went through my mind.

I think there was a feeling as well that this was a middle finger up to Westminster. There was a northern dimension to all this, too. It wasn't just about London deciding how we were going to live our lives and telling us that multi-culturalism was going to work. There was this sense of sending a message to say we had minds of our own and the way we voted was up to us. Maybe that was part of the reason for the result too. I think that Eric was the only really local candidate on the list: the rest weren't exactly from the south-east, but they certainly weren't seen as born and bred. Eric's great strength was appealing to the working-class man, rousing the fire in him. He was respected and he had the right voice; more than that – he had the perfect voice.

But I think I went home that night imagining the place would be back to normal the following morning. That's generally the way of it, isn't it? You can have a right old political earthquake and the next day the bins are still collected and old Mr Jones still walks his poodle to the newsagent's to pick up his copy of the paper. I just thought it had been an exciting night and it went to show you could never predict the outcome of elections. I drew my curtains and paid homage to the patron saint of political upsets. I had no earthly idea what was about to happen. But I would still contend that no one did: not a soul. I'd put money on that.

★

I'M NOT HONESTLY sure how it all began. It's funny how everything's clear at the time and then hardly any time later you start to question the order of things. I was working late that night, was down in one of the side streets where the company has a basement. I'm not the least bit political: I'm one of the silent majority. You have extremists on both sides; each lot is as bad as the other. No doubt they have points to make, but I think the past few months illustrate more than anything what things are like at the edges. The irony is that I used to be very politically engaged once upon a time: I was a Labour man with strong working class roots. Then I lost faith in Labour – I think it was the Iraq war that did it. I marched with the millions against that war and no one listened. That was the last straw: I lost faith in the machines that politicians had become. They weren't people any more. I didn't truly believe they cared. But I especially didn't believe that where I lived, on the edge of Sudburgh. I saw the worst of things over perhaps eighteen months or two years and I felt sickened.

I saw White Rose activists and they made my blood run cold. They were looking for a war and any way they could find to start one. Many of the hangers-on were nothing more than thugs, young men who were bored and didn't know what to do with themselves. I'm sure plenty of the ones I saw weren't even members of the organisation; they were just kids looking for kicks. They might have had White Rose insignia and they might well have had a vague sense of what the group stood for, but why let the facts get in the way of a good fight? I did blame the politicians all the same; I saw them at the root of all this and it sickened me. White Rose had grown out of a dark place in our society, a failure to talk honestly and openly about multi-cultural issues.

On the other hand, you had the Islamic community and I feel I don't have the authority to say much about its members. I'm white and I've grown up in a white working-class world. I've seen both sides. In my street there were good, law-abiding, hard-working Pakistanis who didn't want to fight with anyone, but I'm well aware of the darker side. It's those at the edges on both sides I blame and almost hate. They have done the worst thing of all: they have spread fear. And that fear on both sides *has* spread, slowly but surely, into the moderate community.

So that night of the by-election result I happened to be

in the basement, working out this and that in relation to the business. I'm a self-professed workaholic; always have been, always will be. I love what I do and I find it hard to stop at five o'clock on a Friday evening. Anyway, I came back upstairs having locked up the basement and found it was about one in the morning. I was about to come outside when I heard shouting and stopped. There was a window at the side of the door and from where I was I could see the flames of a bonfire. My first thought was simply to get a sense of what was going on; to be frank, you don't want to mess with bits of Sudburgh on a Saturday night. Don't get me wrong, the place has been all too harshly maligned for years and that's been tough, but the problems are there all the same. I'm just not convinced any of the politicians have done much to address them.

At any rate, I was sort of standing close in to the door in the shadows. I could get a view out of the side window to my left, but it was very much an angled view. Anyway, all of a sudden I saw this group of white kids dragging out an Asian guy somewhere to my left; they were shouting and laughing. The front of the place was brightly lit, so the fact that it was one in the morning was neither here nor there. I remember coming out at a similar time from the basement a few years back and dropping papers on the pavement; I bent to pick them up and was aware that I could read everything clearly under the sharpness of the street lights. So you ask me how I knew they were whites and the guy they had was Asian: I just saw it right away. There wasn't a shadow of doubt.

I could see the whole group clearly; they were shouting and laughing. The Asian was scared; he was shrieking and struggling to get away. They got him down on the ground and two of them were holding open his legs and the third one started kicking him viciously, as hard as he could. He was screaming in pain and the guy just went on kicking him, boot after boot after boot. I felt sick. I felt frightened as well, to be honest; I shrank back into the shadows and could feel myself shaking. I sank right down onto the floor and I heard the kicking going on and on. Eventually the Asian guy vomited and seemed to pass out. The two that had been holding him just dropped him like a doll onto the concrete. I think that was what stunned me most of all: he somehow wasn't a human being to them. It was as if they had been playing a video game and now it was over.

For a second they looked in to where I was crouching, and I was terrified they might break their way in to get me. I don't think they saw me; in fact, I'm certain they didn't. I was just like a frightened rabbit. I crouched there in the shadows until they'd gone off laughing. I can remember wondering just what I believed in as I crept back home. I wasn't sure there seemed much left.

★

'CAN I ASK you to assure us that the situation in Sudburgh is under control?'

'Of course it is under control! Look, I am not going to sit here and deny that the by-election result was a shock and a disappointment, but we have to move on from that. The fact is there are plenty of sane, decent political thinkers both in and around Sudburgh; just because Eric Semple managed to squeeze past the post by the skin of his teeth does not mean that anarchy ensues the following day. I personally felt a profound sense of sadness at the result because it seemed a victory for extremism over reason and partnership, but I believe profoundly it was the result of a protest vote.'

'And yet the fact of the matter is that White Rose are gaining in strength month by month. Doesn't that in itself say something about how people in the street are turning their backs on the mainstream parties? Isn't it a very real sign of failure on the part of leaders like you to address the questions they feel are being put to one side? One of your own backbenchers said that there was a tendency to "bury the difficult questions in unmarked graves". Surely it must worry you that the battle seems to be lost?'

'I am desperately concerned about extremism on both sides. What happened at Burroway did nothing less than break my heart. When I was interviewed that morning at the site I felt I spoke as a husband and a father first, as Prime Minister second. But the fact of the matter is that I don't possess any kind of magic wand to wave away extremism. And I don't believe that anyone does. Perhaps it's akin to putting out a heathland fire. You feel you've done the job and then the smouldering begins over there, and there; you have to go back and beat the ground again and again until you're certain the job's done. And even then you have to keep on watching and watching, being on your guard. But in the end it's about new growth, a green returning through all that's been blackened and burned. It's a long, long process.'

'And what if you're wrong, Prime Minister? What if the heath fire that would seem to be under Sudburgh, and other towns, can't be put out so easily? Will you personally take responsibility for that failure?'

'Let me come back and talk about that in three months' time, or in half a year. I don't believe in failure here – I simply can't afford to do so. I believe that the hard work which has been done over the years in building stronger community relations in that whole area will prevail. I think we must be careful not to be complacent and to see that the hard work has to continue, but let's talk up that hard work, not talk it down. I don't believe that good community relations can be decided just by white papers from government, deep in the Westminster Bubble. I think it's much more about what happens on the ground: how a teacher deals with the bullying of an Asian student, how a local church reaches out to the Pakistani community on its doorstep. It would be wrong and dangerous to put all this at the feet of politicians, and that's not dodging the question or passing the buck.

What we need to believe is that together the rebuilding can and will be done.'

★

*S*EVERAL PETROL BOMBS *were thrown into offices belonging to the White Rose organisation in the centre of Sudburgh earlier this afternoon. Reports suggest that a protest by members of the Asian community was being held outside when scuffles broke out. While police were attempting to restore order, the petrol bombs were thrown through the upper windows of the building. It appears that until today the precise location of the White Rose office was being kept secret for security reasons. A fire at once broke out inside the building and fire crews struggled for over an hour to gain access, before bringing out at least three seriously injured individuals, all believed to be members of White Rose. Eric Semple has appealed for calm, saying that nothing is to be gained from mindless acts of violence in the city, but many of his political opponents accuse him of having said and done far too little to condemn the unrest that has come in the wake of the Sudburgh by-election. Police have confirmed that the fire at the White Rose office was quickly brought under control once access was gained to the building, but they* *have again appealed in the strongest terms to protesters to allow the emergency services immediate access to sites of all kinds when it is necessary. They complain that too often the emergency services are being hampered from doing their work, and that today's events were a perfect example of what was later described as the mindless behaviour of a minority. The local hospital where the three victims of the petrol bomb attack were taken has said that one man with serious burns is fighting for his life.*

★

I'M NOT SURE what I thought. I think I believed I was political, but I had no idea what that really meant. Being political was doing a lot of shouting and breaking a few windows. But I was fired up by Eric Semple, and so were a lot of people. Young guys of my age especially, but I don't think only us. He really said it like it was. You watched Eric Semple speaking – or shouting would be more accurate! – and you felt really excited. Looking back, I'm not actually sure there was a lot he could do. He was one tiny cog in a huge wheel, and apart from making a hell of a lot of noise (which he did), I'm not certain what else there was to do. I remember actually thinking that a few days after he was elected. He'd made so much noise in the lead-up, and then once he was elected he seemed to go quiet. In a way it was perhaps easier shouting from the side-lines, making a protest that everyone heard loud and clear. I think the hard part began once he got there, once he was elected. I don't know, but I remember thinking something of that at the time. Perhaps we did talk politics now and again, but if we did it was most likely just racist rants. It was wishful thinking: we lived boring, miserable lives on council estates doing little but going round in circles. Eric Semple was exciting; he was something else, something worth shouting about. I'm not sure there was any real goal.

There was a white guy on the estate who started dating an Asian girl. He got a lot of warnings but I don't think he cared. I think he was bright, heading for university. Anyway, he was given a last warning, told he had to break it off. Our area was controlled by a group of White Rose members, and they were a bunch you didn't mess with. They helped people they liked who were in trouble, but they also kept an eye on the ones they didn't. It was mostly a case of control by fear. I suspect this guy didn't think they'd actually do anything; I mean, what he was doing was hardly illegal. But they went to his house one night and dragged him out. They told him he'd had all the warnings he needed and hadn't listened. Now it was the fox and hounds: that was the name of the 'game' they played. I hadn't heard of that before then either. They said he had five minutes to run and then they were coming after him. They chased him for well over an hour until he jumped over a bridge and got caught on some railings. They just left him. I believe without a doubt that story's true; they were capable of that kind of thing. In a way they were as bad and worse to whites as they were to Asians or blacks. They forced a lot of kids to join White Rose, especially boys in secondary school. It was about making money, pure and simple.

I didn't actually know any Asians. After what happened to that guy on our estate I wouldn't have wanted to take the risk. In a way you felt there were two levels to White Rose: there were the ones at the top with the public face. Then there were the rest, the kind I saw all around me all the time. It's as if one lot operated through the day and the other lot only once it got dark. I'm sure the ones in charge knew what was going on but they never said anything; they just made sure nothing could ever be proved. In some ways I think they were even more dangerous. The ones down below were pretty much thugs; they were just useful. The ones up above were like actors; they said all the right things and knew how to cover their tracks. But underneath was something else.

★

I SUPPOSE IT would have been about eight o'clock by then: I had rather lost any sense of time. We filed downstairs into this weird mausoleum of a place, and what I remember more than anything is the airlessness. It had been stuffy enough in the interview room, in the modern part of the building; down below at the back of it everything just felt strange and stifling. Perhaps that was all part of the intention. The prisoner really began to show signs of distress on the way down the stairs; he obviously didn't know what on earth was happening and started to panic. For the last hours while we interviewed him I would almost say he had grown confident; he certainly lost any anxiety he'd arrived with. And my colleague and I had effectively been nice to him; he knew that too. So this just seemed to throw him into a complete tail-spin. My superior led the way and my colleague, the officer with whom I'd conducted the interview, came behind him. So the prisoner was between the two of us and we were half holding on to him as we went down the last of the steps. He was looking all around him; I can remember seeing his eyes in the half-darkness of the place. It was musty, it was hot, it was claustrophobic. I don't remember there being any windows; I certainly couldn't see any. You felt below ground there, whether that was true or not. I had that sense of there not being quite enough air to breathe. My boss, my superior officer, call him what you will, drew me to one side as soon as we were down there. He spoke very quietly but looked at me the whole time with fierce eyes and jabbed one finger in the air as he spoke. He said this could be a simple matter of life and death, that he knew exactly what he was doing and believed it was absolutely justified. He said there was no reason for what was going to take place to be mentioned beyond these walls, that he expected my full cooperation as on any other occasion. Then he turned away.

There was a very simple, stark table in the chamber; I don't think there was anything at all in the way of chairs. We were told that we should undress the prisoner and that he should lie on his back on the table. I can remember him looking at me as we obeyed and started taking off his clothes; I think he was quite beyond words with shock, and I could feel his arms trembling as together we pulled off his shirt. I didn't know whether my superior actually intended us to remove his underwear; I just turned round towards him preparing to voice my question and he simply gave a single nod. We then made the prisoner lie down on his back; I'm not sure if he would have done that of his own accord by that stage. I can't honestly remember whether he was making any noise at that point, but he was certainly shaking. I can recall my own heart racing; I felt extremely uncomfortable with the whole situation but had no idea what else to do. I've castigated myself many times for not having spoken or acted in some way to question what was going on. I am well aware that my silence and the silence of my colleague makes us complicit in what took place. I'm not at all sure what we would have done or could have done. All right, I'm sorry, I realise I'm not here to try to justify my actions but simply to record them.

My superior officer stood facing the prisoner at the

bottom of the table, so to speak. I saw that he brought something out of the bag he had carried with him. I couldn't see what it was at that point because of the poor light. He spoke in a very measured way, as though he was absolutely calm. He said he was holding a device in his hands that he now felt compelled to use because of the gravity of the situation. The prisoner had confessed to his part in a terrorist attack on the country that had been responsible for the deaths of over a hundred and sixty innocent people and the injury of many more. The others directly involved in the attack had died in it – they had to all intents and purposes been suicide bombers – and now it was imperative to know who else might have been involved in the planning of the attack, and what other planning may already have been in place for further attacks.

He held up the device and turned it around, but even then I couldn't get any real sense of it because of the lack of light. He said that it would be fitted over the scrotum and gradually tightened, and that it had last been used on an IRA suspect in the 1970s in Northern Ireland. He then fitted the device and it was clear it was intended to feel very tight from the outset – the prisoner certainly reacted when it was put into place. I'm not sure what I felt: a mixture of revulsion and anxiety and pure shock. I have been trained to operate within the law and for over twenty years that is precisely what I have done. I have been all too aware of cases, particularly involving the Metropolitan Police, where the law has been bent for the sake of politicians or indeed for officers. I have found myself deeply ashamed of the evidence that has emerged, or even the crimes that have been supressed. I am all too aware that although officially this country is opposed to the use of torture, it has nevertheless been used. And I'm not simply meaning various types of stress positions that might or might not be described as torture; I'm not meaning these grey areas – I'm speaking of very real, unequivocal uses of torture in Northern Ireland, in Kenya, and doubtless elsewhere too. I'm no expert in the history, but it simply cannot be denied that torture has been used for the extraction of information.

And that was what was happening in front of me, before my eyes. As I've said, I felt a sheer bewilderment of emotions, but I was certainly not quite able to believe the situation. In describing it all to you, as honestly as possible, I have slowed things down quite ridiculously. The truth is that moving from the interview room to the basement, to the beginning of what can only be described as torture, would have taken all of eight minutes. I cannot believe it was longer.

★

OH, I DON'T think anybody in the country realised just how serious things were in Whitehall. I'm not even sure I realised! Perhaps you don't feel the true force of a crisis, if that's the best description, until afterwards. Perhaps something of the PM's panic got through to the tabloids; I think a hint of that was there, certainly. But the truth is that the leader of the opposition didn't have an awful lot to throw at him. I think he realised that himself, and though there was inevitable sparring about soddling Sudburgh – that was what it tended to be known as behind closed doors – it was all quite careful. The opposition knew damn well it was a case of there but for the grace of God. They knew fine the PM was quite right when he said that a magic wand couldn't be waved over such a situation. They might even have gone as far as to feel something like sympathy for what the whole thing had spiralled into. I suppose the London lot – those who couldn't quite see anything north of Watford without a telescope – would have muttered to begin with that it was a case of the tail wagging the dog. Yes, I might have been guilty of that kind of attitude in the first days. The fact was that rather a lot was happening elsewhere in the world – as there always is! – and that we were in danger of spending a disproportionate amount of time worrying about a little idiot in Sudburgh. His nickname up there – sometimes used rather affectionately – was the Little Hitler. I think that was our way of cutting him down to size in Whitehall, by simply slicing that to the little idiot. Because that's effectively what he was. He happened to be able to appeal wildly to the flog 'em and hang 'em brigade, and he made reasonably good speeches. But there was no substance there: what did he think he was going to do about it? He wasn't about to bring in naval vessels to cart off hundreds of thousands of Pakistanis! There's too much of a fondness for curry in his neck of the woods for that to happen anyway. You can just see these White Rose sympathisers having their five pints on a Friday night and then going home with a curry. The whole thing's lunacy, but it was very dangerous lunacy at the time all the same. And the fire-bombing of the White Rose offices marked a very real escalation of it all. I suspect the PM thought that some kind of order had been restored after the election of Eric Semple as MP. They were really praying there wouldn't be any acts of retaliation; all of the imams in the North were being contacted to beg them to use what influence they had. And to give them their due, I think they were doing their best. But it wasn't enough, not nearly enough.

★

I AM A COMMUNITY leader, or at least I was. I'm from the Pakistani community, but I didn't grow up in Sudburgh itself. I would prefer that my name not be given, particularly because of the events of recent months. I see no real reason for my name to be revealed. Thank you for respecting this.

I am partly concerned regarding my identity because I have been involved at various times in political activity. I am not an extremist and I never have been, but I have worked alongside many from my community who were probably radicalised, even though they never spoke openly in those terms. So while I am not a radical, I can find myself having some degree of sympathy with radical ideas and positions. I think what you can say to begin with is that people on both sides are angry. But my community feels more vulnerable. They feel a minority, and often a hated one. They do not understand what they have done wrong. They have worked hard and did not set out to cause trouble. Many feel it is simply the colour of their skin and the difference of their religion that causes the hatred. But are these things really enough for hatred?

And many feel too that what White Rose and other groups want is to make things worse, not better. I have been a community leader, but my work was not only with my own young people. Much of what I did was to bring both sides together, to get them to begin to listen and share. And even though it was often step by small step, it worked. I saw it working and so did other people, even the politicians. But these are the kind of steps that can be destroyed overnight, and I think that made me give up in the end. The sad truth is that what groups like White Rose wanted was war. They did not want good community relations to happen. They wanted to break down the bridges that had been built and prove that this multi cultural society was impossible. And they managed to create more anger on the other side – a great deal more anger – and that was exactly what they hoped would be the result. I believe things could have been done quite differently.

When you watch a youth club that has been built, actually put together bit by bit, burning out of control and to the ground, it makes you very bitter. I have witnessed this twice, and the second time probably made me decide that enough was enough. Of course I do not agree with radicalisation, but I certainly see where the seeds of it lie! And if anything, the politicians have sought to do more for the white communities they think are angry. I ask what about the Asian communities that are hurt and angry, what are you going to do to restore a sense of democracy for them? Because if they do not feel they have genuine democracy then they will reach for radical solutions. Surely the first is better than the second.

I have been told several times by young white men that I should go home. I was born and brought up in this part of England, but of course I know that they mean Pakistan. I have no home there, but sometimes I wish that I could leave and begin a better life there. I believe it would be harder, but I cannot believe it would be any less happy. It could not be. I do not believe that multi-culturalism has failed: I believe it has been made to fail. And I believe that is far more sad.

★

I'M THE DAUGHTER of Eric and Trish Semple and I have also asked that my own name not be revealed. Yes, I know that has been accepted, but I would like to explain my reasons. No, that is my right and I would like to begin by explaining my reasons! I have felt myself to be in danger over the past months and I do actually have police protection and very much feel the need for it. I am not living in the Sudburgh area for obvious reasons and have been back there on only a couple of occasions as my evidence will reveal. I have found that difficult because I grew up in a very close and loving home, and particularly because of what has happened to my family over these months. I'm sorry, I'll be fine. Yes, I will continue. I want to continue. I just find having to talk about all this in detail very hard indeed.

I was with my family on the evening after the bombing of the White Rose place in town. I was actually trying to work for an exam and managing to get peace was almost impossible because the phone was ringing the whole time. What was my father like? I would say he was under a hell of a lot of pressure. I remember him quite changed after he was elected MP. I don't actually think he ever expected it would happen. I'm not even sure now if he wanted it to happen. I don't know for sure if that's true and I would say I think it's impossible to know. I didn't talk to him much about politics; I think me and my brother just got sick of the whole thing and simply wanted our dad back. It just felt like he was an ordinary guy. I think a lot of my friends had very little relationship with their parents and that was a surprise to me; I couldn't understand it. We had grown up very close and I felt both my parents were friends. That's what makes it so hard for me. Yes, I apologise. No, I don't need a break – it's fine.

But I feel I did lose touch with him a lot over that year. I think it felt as if he was a lot angrier, if that makes any sense? I don't mean angrier with us, angrier with the world. He read a hell of a lot and was away at least one day most weeks. I think it's the first time I really remember he and my mum falling out big time; they had always got on – they just seemed great friends, and that changed. As I say, he seemed angrier and possibly more nervous. *Anxious* might be a better word. I think some of that may just have been the strain of long days doing political stuff. But I think he also knew he was taking a real risk standing for so much of what White Rose wanted.

I really don't believe he saw himself as one of them. Of course, I can't be sure of that, but it's what I believe all the same. I've fallen out with my brother about this because he doesn't agree, but it's my opinion. I don't believe my dad ever wanted what did happen in the end to happen at all. And I go back to what I said earlier on: I'm not even convinced he wanted to win the by-election. I think he wanted to give them a fright and get a good result; I believe he wanted to make them think. But that was it. He did speak about it being all over soon: I can remember him saying that to my mum. It was as if he wanted things to be back to normal himself. This was going to be his political bit and then he'd go back to being Eric Semple. Yes, I will take a break if you don't mind. I'm sorry; I apologise. I'll be fine, but I'll take a break.

★

TWO LARGE FIRES are raging out of control tonight on the edge of Sudburgh. It's not known how they started, but police believe that tensions are simply running high after the attack on the White Rose buildings in the centre of the city. The fires, which are believed to be visible from a distance of several miles, may have been started by groups of youths who are supporters of White Rose. One of the men severely burned in the attack on the Sudburgh office, Terry Radcliffe, died some hours ago as a result of his injuries.

A spokesman for White Rose has said that a march in his memory is to be organised for this coming Saturday, though police have not yet confirmed that permission has been given for the march to pass through a predominantly Asian area of Sudburgh. The police have again appealed for calm tonight following widespread incidents of looting and violence experienced for several nights now. In a joint statement, members of the Church of England and representatives from the Muslim Council of Britain have said that neither religion tolerates violence or the perpetration of acts of hate or revenge. They have appealed to White Rose to abandon any plans for a march through the city, saying that this would simply risk exacerbating an already severely troubled state in Sudburgh and in the region as a whole. They say that instead a joint service of prayers for reconciliation will be held on Sunday, though it has not been decided where this will take place. Let's speak to our reporter, Dennis Bradley, who's in Sudburgh city centre this evening...

★

As I said before, I was working for an exam that night and I wasn't in a great mood. That's one of my regrets now; that's something that will always live with me, the fact that I snapped at my dad. I reckon he must have put the phone off about nine o'clock; I think my mum couldn't take any more of it and this was the first real bit of quiet all evening. I had just started to concentrate and get down to things when he came in and asked me if I wanted a cup of tea. I know it was kindly meant but I just burst into flames and told him to leave me alone. It was the stress of everything, I suppose, but I knew I needed to pass this exam and that it counted for a great deal. Then afterwards you weigh things up and ask yourself what really matters, and had I known anything of what was going to happen I would never have reacted that way. I know, I'm sorry, I realise I'm leaving the actual story, but this is important all the same! I'm not just some machine that can spew out the facts and leave feelings to one side.

I remember my Dad going; he just closed the door very quietly behind him and didn't say any more. I do actually remember looking up at the clock not many minutes later because I wanted to have a sense of how much longer I could work for. I had a digital clock on a shelf and I remember it was 21.13. I have no idea exactly how long would have passed then; it might have been twenty minutes, half an hour. I went out to the loo at that point – so you could say it was somewhere between half past nine and quarter to ten – and that's when it happened. I really remember the silence there was at that point, I suppose because of the noise there had been beforehand. It was as though I'd shut the whole world up. There was just nothing.

The front door burst open and these two masked figures came into the hall. They were screaming all the time and I think they were armed. It's so hard to know these things afterwards; you're in such a state of shock and everything happens so fast. No idea if I was screaming or not; I do know that I just sank down there at the top of the stairs. I had this sense of wanting to make myself as small as possible, of wanting to go into a kind of ball. They were banging open doors and screaming; I think I could hear my mum shrieking in the living room. And then they simply dragged my dad out. I saw that happening down below me; I think I had my face half in my hands like a child, but I saw it all clearly. That's the strange thing: he didn't seem to put up any kind of resistance at all. I don't know, it was as if he knew it was going to happen, or was prepared for it at any rate. They were dragging him and dragging him, but it was actually all totally unnecessary. I think he would have walked out the front door with them if they'd asked him to.

And just as they got there it was as if he knew I was there, as though he sensed me at the top of the stairs. He turned his face round and looked up and our eyes met for just a flash. I can remember exactly how his face looked, his expression, but I'll never know exactly what it meant, how to interpret it. I thought for a long time there was fear there, but I don't know. I've wondered if it was also a kind of sadness, a sort of asking for forgiveness. I'm sure fear was part of it, but I don't believe it was everything either. Then it was over and he was dragged out the door. It was as though everything happened in a matter of seconds after that. The moment when he looked at me felt as though it lasted for ever; it was all a kind of slow motion. Then the door was just slammed shut and I heard the car outside humming away. It wasn't like in some kind of clichéd film with the squealing of tyres and all that; it was just this humming and then dead silence.

Total and absolute silence. And just the soft, soft sound of my mum crying.

★

IT WAS ALMOST the quiet before the storm that night, I suppose. I came back to Sudburgh about three in the morning; I'd been visiting friends in the Lake District and we'd actually been out walking – long days in the fells. Sorry, I haven't introduced myself – my name is Kevin Langley and I work as a GP in a practice on the edge of Sudburgh. I've been asked to give evidence because of the community I serve, and I suppose to shed light on things from that perspective. Is that sufficient?

As I say, I was coming back to Sudburgh in the middle of the night, and I wasn't actually aware of what had happened in the city earlier that day. I think these friends had almost dragged me away to give me a break. Not so much from the politics, more from the drugs and the sheer sadness of the place! I shouldn't say *the place* actually, because that's giving a dog a bad name. There's Sudburgh and there's Sudburgh. Every area is the same. It so happens that my district – or at least the district where the practice is – has to be one of the worst, or you might say one of the parts that faces the most severe problems. Sorry, but I think that's worth clarifying.

But as I said, I was totally unaware of the bomb attack on the White Rose place earlier that day. We had had the television off for four days and there was no way I was going to listen to the radio on the way back. I had on classical music; I can't remember for the life of me what it was. I was heading to my surgery first to pick up a copy of the next day's schedule and the place was just absolutely dead. There wasn't anyone about and I can't remember seeing any cars. Normally there's a joyrider or two, especially in the part where my practice is – but there was just nothing. It was quite eerie, especially because you could see the remains of bonfires everywhere. I saw one burned-out car and I can remember slowing down to look at it. I can remember it was half up on the pavement, as though the driver had driven up there, got out, and then the car had been torched.

I felt it was like being in a film. There was just a ghostliness about the place, as though something was about to happen. You kept waiting but nothing did happen. I was very awake; I felt absolutely wide awake, even though I'd been walking that morning and had then driven back, even though it was now well after three.

I saw just one face that whole time, at an upper window. It was the face of a girl, watching me. I've no idea how old she would have been. She was Asian and very beautiful; I was driving really slowly and able to look up for longer than the split second you'd usually have. It sounds stupid, but it was that that made me realise the place was alive after all, that it wasn't dead. It just all felt so abandoned. There were White Rose symbols painted here and there; they shone out in the darkness, and that was eerie too. It felt like that was the intention. Everything else was just grey, the whole place. And they were almost like eyes, watching.

I got home shortly after seeing that girl's face and I learned immediately what had happened earlier in the day. Not just that, I got a sense of what all the past days had been like. And perhaps I got a sense too of what was likely to lie ahead.

★

I DO REMEMBER the moment I heard about Eric Semple; I think many people will do. I was working up in my attic that morning and had the radio on. It was a very warm day and the heat of the attic was quite oppressive. We'd had a burst pipe and I was basically cleaning up a section of flooring that had got soaked. I wasn't actually listening to the radio at all; it was just on in that kind of background way – a mixture of talk and song, a way of filling the quiet. Yeah, I think I'd call it Pollyfilla for the silence! And then I suddenly realised what was being said; it was as if the dials suddenly turned the voice sharp and I just sat there, on my hands and knees, not quite able to believe what I was hearing. That Eric Semple had been abducted by masked men late the previous night, that he had been driven off in a car without registration plates – a car that was later abandoned. And that police were appealing for any information that might help them with their inquiries. It took time just to absorb the words, to understand what they meant.

And then the radio seemed to return to being a blur. I just sat there, with the echo of what had been said repeating and repeating in my head. There was no doubt that tensions were high, but I don't think anyone could have foreseen that. And it's a mark of our democracy that there was no guard on his house. There were all sorts of outcries afterwards, that that was what he should have had to begin with. But the fact is that nobody expected it; no one even saw it as a possibility. And that says a great deal about the democratic process in this country. The fact was that he had been elected fair and square. And in this country we don't deal with the things we dislike by assassinating people or abducting them.

I went out later on and everyone seemed to be talking about it, although that's perhaps because it was the only thing that was in my head. I don't think it was about anger or grief; I think it was simply shock. That this could happen in Sudburgh. As much as anything it was just numbness, a sort of disbelief. And I don't remember seeing a single White Rose badge either. It was just about ordinary people being shocked and going about their lives as though on tiptoe. The silent majority. I think there was sorrow for his family; I got the sense of that more than anything. A sort of helplessness, a feeling of not quite knowing what to do. I think most people kept on hoping it would all be over in the city. It had been one thing after another and with every lull people hoped it might come to an end. And I think I'm in a position to know. I work as a taxi driver in the city centre and many people end up talking about all of that. Usually it's the drivers who get the blame for initiating it, but I've long since been too careful to talk politics in my neck of the woods! I'd rather talk about the weather. No, the boot's on the other foot for sure. People want to get something off their chest; they're in the back and they can't see your face and so they talk more openly than they might anywhere else. I say sometimes I should be a Roman Catholic priest. They're coming for a kind of confession. Not because of what they've done wrong so much as what the world has done wrong. It's a way of working out the world. And me? The safest thing to do's agree with everyone. It may sound like cowardice, but late on a Saturday night and heading out to a Sudburgh estate, it feels very much like wisdom to me.

★

I WAS DRAFTED in for the White Rose protest. I'm in the police and it's about keeping law and order, and at times you end up doing things you don't particularly like. You can't pick and choose, any more than a fireman can decide whether or not he likes the look of the blaze he's been asked to put out. No, but my point is a serious one. You can't argue with the uniform; you have to maintain a neutrality to the very best of your ability. If I'm absolutely pushed on a personal level I would say that I had been quite disgusted by what had been allowed to happen. I felt it had all spun out of control and it was time for some kind of order to be restored. I don't mean that actually in terms of law and order – although inevitably that's part of it – I mean it far more in respect of the politics. I think basically we had a weak Prime Minister. I felt that nothing had happened over Burroway except that we had decided to build a memorial garden. We hadn't even attempted to get to the root cause of what was a major terrorist attack. Did we know why it had happened? Were we urgently seeking to ensure that such a thing was impossible in the future? And now Sudburgh was in danger of becoming an independent republic where extremists on both sides could effectively do what they liked. I was hardly alone in thinking there was something seriously wrong with the message that was being sent out by our so-called government. But I'm saying all this because I'm almost being forced to do so. And I am revealing my personal viewpoint precisely because of my anonymity here today. I simply would not do so otherwise. I think I've probably already said more than I should have done.

On to facts. I think we expected perhaps ten thousand might march that Saturday, but of course after the fire-bombing of the White Rose building Eric Semple was abducted. No one saw that coming. And even though he wasn't officially a representative of that organisation, he was very much singing from their hymn sheet. So that was underestimated and we did get it wrong. I don't think it was a disaster, but I will admit that it could have been. There was a lot of blaming of the police in the post mortem and I simply feel a great deal of that blame is unjustified. You do not have an instruction manual given to you before such events. You work on your best instincts at the time and in the middle of developing situations you simply make decisions that feel justified. Of course you are acting at times out of a need for sheer self-preservation. We are policemen and women out there; we are not machines! It is far too easy to become wise after the event. But I am admitting that mistakes were made, and sometimes those mistakes were serious. I do believe that lessons will have to be learned. Of course I do.

★

W E'RE LOOKING DOWN on the march from the helicopter and at this point it's simply not possible for
me to see the northern end of the numbers – the starting
point of it all. There's a sheer sea of White Rose insignias;
many marchers are wearing armbands with the distinctive
logo and there are quite a number of banners. Many are
bearing the name of Terry Radcliffe, of course. But what
has surprised me is the number of women. White Rose has
often been characterised as a group for working-class men
who don't work. Here today you see the sheer volume of
support there is across the spectrum. And I feel that if I
were to be able to open one of the windows and shut out
the roar of the helicopter blades, I'd be able to hear the
chanting of Eric Semple's name. Because this is perhaps
as much and more about fury over the disappearance, the
kidnapping, of the recently elected member of parliament
as it is about the cause of White Rose – or indeed about
the tragic death of Terry Radcliffe. Many banners bear the
name of Eric Semple, and many display the names underneath of groups who're marching today to remember him,
to demand that even now he's released unharmed.

And it's quite apparent that businesses owned by
people, by ordinary men and women from the Pakistani
and the wider Asian community, have been boarded up
and even reinforced by whole walls of protective material.
Now there, just below us, you can see that implements
of various kinds are being taken to a less well-protected
shop front. And someone is being dragged out; there are
no fewer than four white men setting into the individual

who came out to defend the property! He is being battered repeatedly and is down on the ground – and there is simply no evidence whatsoever of the police! Another window has been smashed and the shop front is being looted. White Rose issued a warning to its members early this morning to say in no uncertain terms... And the violence being meted out to that one man is quite sickening; the images will be clear for all to see. And more has broken out on the far side! It's hard for me to make it out because of the glare, but some kind of barricade is being torn down and now we can see the wall of riot police. They are being attacked from that side by a hail of missiles. And this is the effective mid-point of the march, I would judge. Now some marchers are turning back – those who were already beyond the point of the first instance of violence and looting. The police are simply too few in number and there on the right you can see a group of officers that has been effectively cut off from the rest. They're slashing with their batons and several people are down on the ground – it's hard to tell which side they belong to. One is being jumped on and even from up here you can see the blood. This is quite sickening; this is what you feel was feared to an extent by both sides of the divide. The middle of the march has become little more than a battlefield. Order is going to have to be restored very quickly before this turns into nothing less than a bloodbath. And I'm just hearing ... we're being ordered out of the skies and will report again if and when that's possible. It seems most unlikely and I will hand back now to the studio...

★

T HE THING YOU had to realise was that Eric might not have been kidnapped by Asians to begin with. I think that fact was almost completely overlooked from the outset. The assumption always was that this is what it would have been, but there is absolutely no evidence to back that up.

I'm a friend of the Semple family, have been for more years than I care to remember. There never was any political dimension, if you like, to that friendship. I was actually godfather to their son in the end, even though Eric always maintained stridently that he was an avowed atheist and neither needed nor wanted godparents. Trish was the one who was keen that both children should be baptised, and I'll not inflict that long story on you – there's no need. Suffice to say that our two families remained very close until and through the time of my divorce about eight years ago; they were a great support to me personally, and that would have been about the time Eric was becoming more engaged in political activities. But as I've made clear, this was never about that political world. Our friendship was much older than that, and it was just a very ordinary, solid connection.

I came to the house probably about twelve hours after Eric had been taken. The place was crawling with police; it was just a horrible atmosphere. They were in and out of the front rooms and on the stairs; you could hear radio mikes round you and even the garden was being crawled over for any shred of evidence. I'm sure they were merely doing everything they had to do, but it was just a most unpleasant, nerve-racking atmosphere, and I simply brought Trish and her daughter in to one of the back rooms, which was a kind of refuge from the chaos at the front. We just sat down together and cried; we held on to each other for the next half-hour and wept. I should say that their son was still away at university at that point – my godson – so it was just the three of us. And I remember Trish pouring out this story about a dream she'd had, a nightmare, and that she'd known all along that this was going to happen. She was completely beside herself, and the only thing you can do in a moment like that is be there. You feel that anything you say is next to useless, but in point of fact what matters most is just being there.

I don't think we talked about the kidnapping at all; no, let me take that back, because inevitably we would have done. I'm not sure that I did much but listen; it was Trish who poured out what had happened the night before. It was all just very much at random and then she tried to get her daughter to speak about where she had been at the time and what she had seen. It was clear the girl didn't want to talk at all, wasn't actually *able* to talk. At some point a policewoman came in to the room and talked to both of them; I have to say I was very impressed with the way that woman handled things. It wasn't that she shoved me out of the way in the least; I remember she just sat down on the floor close to them and spoke softly, really tried to be there for them. I was over at the window at that point and I remember a helicopter going over, and I had never seen one so low. It suddenly hit me that Eric was really gone, that he might be dead already. Somehow the whole thing hadn't been quite real before then and it just seemed to wash right over me at that point.

The word I want to use is *drenched*; I somehow felt drenched with the reality of it and was quite emotional myself. I found myself thinking of all manner of things Eric and I had got up to over the years; he was the kind of guy who just inspired. He was somehow a leader; you wanted to be part of his world. I remember on one occasion when he and I broke into a table-tennis club in the middle of the night. I don't even remember where it was. We were far from sober but there was no malevolence in what we did; it was just out of a sheer and crazy sense of adventure. He happened to know where this club was and we managed to get in the back door about three in the morning. Oh, Eric knew all about opening doors; he had years of experience! And we just played table tennis for the next couple of hours; we were both pretty good, and we played our hearts out. We shut the place up again about five in the morning and walked home having sobered ourselves up. That was the kind of thing we did. And it hit me then that I might never be able to laugh with him again about that kind of night. Then I looked over and saw Trish and her girl, and I thought how much worse it was for them.

What I thought about Eric himself? I'm not sure I thought it back then, but perhaps even by that day I was beginning to think a lot about what he had done, what he had set in motion. I've said the whole political thing was never there; the two families were just friends on a very ordinary, human level. I don't think I understood what all that meant to him. I think I felt he had put a hell of a lot on the line for the sake of his views. It just didn't seem worth it; I think it all seemed very selfish. Yeah, I can even remember feeling angry about it. You go through a whole range of emotions and that was certainly one of them. What right had he to sacrifice his family for his beliefs, however important they might have been to him? And I do still find myself thinking that even now, from time to time, despite the fact it's only one of many conflicting feelings, inevitably. I do struggle to understand what he was doing.

★

MY MEMORY OF that time in the basement is somewhat in slow motion, too. I felt in shock; I was just completely thrown by what was happening and by what

I had been asked to do. You wonder afterwards why you didn't act differently, and I can say only that I've done so countless times. On a number of occasions I've woken up in the middle of the night, gasping for breath and just sweating profusely, and the last frame, as it were, of my dream or nightmare, is of standing looking down at our prisoner lying there naked on the bench.

Of course I'm familiar with the device; it was constructed so that it hugged the whole genital area. And I've already stated that it was fitted so as to give a maximum sense of constriction from the outset. The whole business is about fear, generating fear. I don't actually believe – and I feel quite certain of this – that the device was tightened at any point during the interrogation, however long that lasted. I saw no evidence of that and I genuinely believe that that was going to happen only as a last resort. It was all about maximising fear. It comes down to whether or not you believe that to be acceptable.

I can remember standing there with my colleague opposite me and our superior talking and talking to the prisoner about that basement chamber. He said that no one else knew we were there, that it was a place that was completely disused. He said it was completely sound-proofed, that no one would hear him screaming; no one would come to find him. He said that no one knew anyway that he was alive, that they believed all of the terrorists had been killed on the train. He did it well; he did it really well. I did not want to be there myself; I felt quite sick. I had to keep reminding myself that this guy there in front of me had been prepared to bomb a train, to kill and maim hundreds of totally innocent people. I had to tell myself that somehow what was being done now was justified because of the other lives it might save. I don't know if I truly believed that; it's what I told myself then, and not once but many times. All I can say is that I tried to believe it then. Somehow it wasn't even a choice.

Do I believe that no one else knew what was going on? I've also asked myself that question many times, and I reckon it must have been known about. I've thought about how the device was obtained and I've thought about this question of who actually did know the prisoner was still alive. And I've realised that it's possible it wasn't even my superior's decision to carry out this interrogation – call it what you will. That it may have been sanctioned, it may have been ordered, much higher up the chain of command. Beyond that I know nothing, but of course I realise there is every possibility of that being the case.

How long did the whole thing last? After all the years of training I've had and after however much experience, I'm ashamed to say that I simply don't know. I am aware how that must come across and I'm sorry. But I say again that I felt I was somehow operating in slow motion; I was just aware of being there in that dark and breathless basement, watching this guy thrashing about on the bench below me. If you insist on some kind of answer, I'd say minutes. I said before that I reckoned it must have taken all of eight minutes to get from the interview room on the upper floor to the beginning of the interrogation in the basement. And then it was perhaps another five or ten minutes. Yes, it would have been as little as that.

My superior was just quiet in the end; he simply stood there at the end of the bench and I remember he had his arms folded. The prisoner was gabbling; it was just a torrent of stuff I could hardly make out, about some idea or other that had to do with a base. He kept using the word *base*, but so much of what he said was just a mumbled torrent – he was barely coherent. Then my boss went and crouched beside him and said very quietly that he was going to tighten the device and the prisoner shrieked; he just jerked like a doll a single time and flipped over and fell off the bench. He must have had a seizure, some kind of massive seizure, and he just landed on the floor completely still.

★

I WON'T FORGET that afternoon as long as I live. I was twenty-four and had been working in casualty for only six months. I felt as if I was in some kind of war zone. I'd find myself thinking this wasn't real, it was something invented by central government to give us training in some kind of nightmare pandemic scenario. I think the worst period would have been between two and three in the afternoon. Hideous injuries. A man whose face had been stamped to a pulp, and pretty much the rest of him jumped on too. A whole number of people with burns; they were easier to deal with, but they were in a great deal of pain, and I hadn't really seen burns before. The place was simply chaos. You go into automatic pilot; I literally worked through into the small hours of the next day. I do feel the whole unit became a team that night, in a way it had never been before. I have thought of that subsequently, that I feel a kind of kinship with those who were working that day. But I have no earthly wish to idealise it now and forget just how hellish it was at the time. Of course there's a danger of that. I don't think that anything television can simulate can get close to the reality of a day like that. There were quite a number of White Rose supporters by then. I think by that stage the Asian community had had enough; as they saw it the time had come to defend themselves. I stress that is supposition on my part; I'm a doctor, and the politics at the back of all this simply makes me angry. You stand there and feel that none of this has to be. I do remember that at about four in the morning there was a bit of a lull; I went out for a cup of tea and a few minutes of air. There was a woman in the waiting area whose son was in intensive care; he'd been stabbed, but he was going to pull through all right. She was just beyond tiredness, sitting in one of those plastic seats all hunched in to herself and crying.

Some people cry to attract attention; often children do that. But this was just a soft and slow crying that tore at your heart. I don't think I've ever thought of crying as beautiful before, but I did at that moment. I stood there and thought that I'd done everything possible to try to help her son, that the only other thing I could do was to give her a hug. Of course, that's probably breaking every single rule in the book, but sometimes you have to throw the book out of the window. I just sat beside her and gave her a hug, and I remember her looking out at the growing dawn. The sky was red and of course it made me think of blood, and I realised there would probably be more victims coming in before it was over. And just at that moment I felt like crying myself. I thought this was all so pointless and tragic, and that the only thing I could do was to try to put faces back together. Those were the words that came to me as I looked out at the dawn: the only thing I could do was to try to put faces back together. And it didn't matter whose they were; it wasn't for me to be on one side or the other. I was in the middle, seeing past badges and insignia and veils and the rest of it. I felt very helpless at that moment; I think I was just beyond myself, to be honest, but I somehow felt the pain of the whole situation. I think I had a sense too almost of anger, that politicians don't have to carry the real weight of suffering. They had brought this into being, on both sides, but then they had walked away.

★

I SUPPOSE I would have been there in all for about two hours; it might have been longer. Basically I had been up in the Sudburgh area for a bike show and I was going home that day. I had no idea this march was taking place and I literally walked right into the middle of it. That is the honest truth. A lot of my London friends were simply incredulous – not because they didn't believe me or thought I was making it up, but because they couldn't get over the fact that I didn't know there was going to be this massive march!

We had been at a pub outside Sudburgh the night before and it had turned into a pretty heavy session. I was the only one actually up some time around noon. I had promised my girlfriend I would be back in London that evening and I simply got my stuff and went. I was on my way to the bus station and I ran right across the path of the march. I literally banged straight into the middle of it, came out of a side street and found myself in the wild west. It was really bizarre. I was hungover and going through all these back streets, happy to have a bit of quiet, and without any warning I was just out into a war zone. I was actually scared witless for the first few minutes, and I'm not exactly the kind of guy that normally is: I'm a biker and I'm power-fully built. I'd happily hammer someone if I think they're out of order, and I've done it many times in the past.

And right beside me was this guy tearing off a Muslim woman's veil. He had a knife and at some point he must have stabbed her; whether it was before I got there or after I don't know. Everything's a blur at a time like that, and even more so if you've just blundered into it! At any rate, I grabbed him and put his lights out. I think it was just a single punch and that was him down, but I reckon that someone must have got me at that point because I found myself on the ground and just realised something was seriously wrong. I felt absolutely no pain, that's the strange thing. I still felt weirdly out of things because of the night before. It's a bit like feeling you're wrapped in cotton wool; the world goes on operating all round you, but you feel strangely absent. So I found myself down on the ground and not feeling the slightest thing, and I realised I was holding the hand of the Muslim woman. I can remember thinking how tiny it was. That was the only thing in my head. It's strange how clear and calm my thinking was. The place was just mayhem round me, and yet I felt this curious sense of well-being, somehow that everything was going to be all right. And then I realised, however much later it was, that the woman's grip had lessened. Her hand was cold.

★

*T*HIRTEEN PEOPLE ARE *now confirmed dead after the violence that broke out during a march organised by the militant right-wing organisation White Rose through the centre of Sudburgh earlier this afternoon. Police fear the death toll may rise as sporadic violence has continued in some side streets and in several housing schemes where the organisation has been particularly active over the past year in the wake of the Burroway bombing. Many community leaders are still expressing their dismay and disbelief that the march, supposedly in memory of Terry Radcliffe from White Rose, was ever allowed to take place. There is still no progress in the hunt for Eric Semple, abducted from his house by masked men late on Thursday evening. No group has claimed responsibility for the kidnapping, and the police continue to stress that there is no conclusive evidence that this was the work of any militant Islamic network established to counter the activities of White Rose. The police have been severely criticised by community leaders in Sudburgh for what they describe as a woefully inadequate response to today's march. They claim that for a time the situation was completely out of control, and maintain that no real attempt was made to shield members of the Asian community, who were left feeling utterly vulnerable. It does seem apparent that for a time the situation was totally chaotic. George Macbeth, who has worked with rival gangs in Sudburgh over the past fifteen years, described the city centre as reminiscent of a scene from a horror movie. He has called on the Prime Minister to visit the city as a matter of urgency, to* *reassure groups on both sides of the divide that measures will be taken to 'heal a wound that has bled too long', as he expressed it. Tonight there are renewed fears of violence, though police have stressed that the city centre itself is absolutely safe. It is still very much closed to traffic, but it is expected that most side streets will be open as normal tomorrow morning.*

★

THERE'S NO DOUBT it was a crisis, that there was a sense of panic in government. All this evidence is being heard in secret and I still – despite the passage of time – wouldn't be revealing all this otherwise. I think that's as much from a sense of loyalty as anything. You're so conditioned to keeping things within the walls of Whitehall, so terribly aware of the possibility of leaks. It's actually, by and large, what I will describe as a watertight environment. And thank God for that; it's simply the way it should be and has to be! What I'm saying is that even though that particular crisis has now passed, my in-built sense of loyalty, of tight-lippedness, so to speak, is still very much there. All right, I've seen that you've got the message, and I'll seek to be as open as I possibly can be.

I think the worst of it was knowing, or not knowing, what to do next. I was part of the Cabinet, and the Cabinet was totally divided. One or two – and I'm sorry but I'm not going to reveal names – wanted to send in the army. I was absolutely opposed to that. I believe it would have acted as a recruiting sergeant to both sides. There's no doubt that the militant Islamic groups were on the point of galvanising their forces. Yes, I do believe they had access to weapons and to bomb-making equipment. There is a report that was prepared by MI5 at the time, and which provides ample evidence; I'd be happy to provide the relevant sections, though I can't supply the document in its entirety. I think the reasons for that are obvious. If you want to take that further then you will have to deal with MI5.

One need only look back to the days of the Troubles in Northern Ireland to see that the army became more of a target than a deterrent. I think we've come a fair distance since then; I like to hope some lessons have been learned. The problem on the other hand was that the worst elements of White Rose had been let out of their cages; I'm afraid that's how we perceived it. It was clear the leadership had little or no control over their activities: you have the age-old problem of reasonably well-educated leaders and a membership that's composed mainly of thugs. I accept it's a crass generalisation, but let's call it a useful shorthand instead. Certainly it's the case that you have a membership composed of some genuine believers in the cause, and some who are there because it beats watching television on a Saturday night. Again, look at Northern

Ireland. The question for the leadership of White Rose was no different in many ways from the question posed to us: how do you reach that following? And for us it was most certainly: how do you go about pacifying that following?

Finally, I think that Enoch Powell was actually absolutely right: you send some people home. That may sound impossible and ridiculous, but I don't think it is. You certainly send home those who have committed criminal offences, and I mean transgressed the law in even the most limited of ways. And you offer incentives to others to leave. I think that would send out very clear and valuable messages to both sides. I think immigrants would cease to think of this country as a soft touch, and the fact is that they do so at present. And I believe that the intelligent elements of White Rose would be pacified, at least to some extent. Of course it wouldn't go far enough for many of them, but it might well take a healthy amount of wind from their sails. I believe education, by the way, is the other half of that particular challenge, but much tougher legislation about criminal activity, past and present, would be more than valuable as a first step. Why hasn't it been introduced? Well, that's a good question. I fear that a decent answer might take at least the best part of a day to provide.

★

I THINK I didn't sleep for three whole nights: I mean, I think I didn't actually sleep for a single moment of those first three nights. I was given medication in the end and I *did* sleep, though I didn't really feel it made any difference. I'm sorry, I was assuming you all knew my name and didn't need any formal introduction. I'm Patricia Semple and Eric was my husband.

I did actually feel from the beginning – I mean, after the time he was taken from the house – that it was all over. I just felt within myself that he wouldn't come back alive. And yes, a lot of that did come down to the dream I'd had. I think once before in my life, right back when I was a teenager, I'd had a dream about a fire and a member of my family being burned. I never said a word about it afterwards and it happened pretty much as I had seen it. So that was only once, but this dream or vision or whatever you want to call it had been so vivid. Even if I think about it now I can see individual faces. It was like a photograph; it was as though a photograph had been slotted into my head. I was somehow there, standing at the back of this underground room. I felt that I could see people but that they couldn't see me. My children still don't know anything about this: I saw no real reason to share it with them at the time – it would have felt far more like inflicting it on them. I think that Eric *did* believe me, it was just too late by then. He had come so far and given so much. I'm not sure that it's true that he didn't *believe* he could win; I think it's more he didn't even *care* whether he won or not. He had somehow

115

burned through to something else, and I realise that doesn't make a lot of sense. He had changed so much in that time. So it's not a case of him not having believed me; it's more that it didn't matter. In a terrible way it was too late. He had to see this through. He wanted to make people think: that was always at the heart of what he believed. He didn't want people blindly marching and putting up barricades – and I certainly don't believe he wanted people resorting to violence. Not before everything else possible had been tried.

Anyway, yes, I apologise. I had shared the dream with one close friend. I suppose I almost regretted it; it had been that first day when the police were swarming over the place and they didn't need me any more. This friend just took me away for an hour or so – to get me away from myself, if you like. And actually it didn't work like that. I just poured out the whole thing, all about Eric and the things that had happened in the past. I must have talked for over two hours and in fact it did a hell of a lot of good. I came back to the house able to face the police again, able to look at the kids.

And then on the morning of the fourth day she just arrived and said she was going to drive me around; we were going to look for the place I'd seen. I didn't even quite understand what she *meant* to begin with; I had never really thought of that place I'd seen in the dream as somewhere you could *look* for. I left a brief note for the kids; told them who I was going with so there would be no worry, and we just drove. I think it was a comfort simply knowing someone else believed me. She didn't actually say whether she did or not, but she certainly believed it was worth doing. She had thought herself about places it might be, and we basically drove for what seemed like hours. I don't suppose it matters, but it might have been an hour and a half. And we got out of the car now and again to have a look at places, and I just didn't *feel* anything was right. It's impossible to explain what I mean by that, but it's really the only way I can express it. Perhaps the best way I've ever felt I could describe it is feeling like you're a metal detector; when you get close to something or when you're right over it you just know.

Sudburgh was still in a state of shock after what had happened on the day of the march, and before it. There were banners carrying Terry's name, but there were plenty with Eric's too. They were hanging from windows, often with a white rose painted in one corner. I remember feeling that the whole city was in mourning for Eric. I don't mean that to sound arrogant or self-obsessed – I'm not sure what the best word would be. It was actually a kind of comfort; it just meant a lot to know he was remembered. I had been in that house and felt so alone, especially during the nights. Of course I talked to the kids, but I also had to hold myself together. I had to.

Anyway, we came to this field on the edge of town and there was something there; I could see something up by the fence but it was too far away to make it out properly. And I just called for her to stop the car because I knew it was there; I knew we were close.

It wasn't a nice area: there was a lot of rubbish and dog mess. I remember seeing needles; I'm always terrified of standing on one. And neither of us had on the right footwear, but we climbed over a fence and started walking. There was a block of flats to one side and we could see people watching us from the balconies. Yes, it did seem as though it was an Asian district – we both had that impression. And there were just these concrete steps going down into the ground. I've no idea what the place had been or why it was still there. There was a kind of overhang; I'm not sure I can describe it accurately. I suppose it felt like an old bomb shelter. There was just broken glass, a lot of mess; the concrete was cracked and grass was growing up through it. And we went underneath, right down below this overhang and inside. And then I just stood in that one spot and I knew I was exactly where I had been in the dream. But I knew I had been wrong about one thing. It hadn't happened; it was still waiting to happen.

★

'WE ARE HERE today to remember those who have died over the past days of violence here in Sudburgh. We have come neither to condemn nor condone: we have come to remember the victims. Not only the fifteen who have now died, but the many others who are still fighting for their lives in hospital, some of whom will be disfigured for life. We are here in a Christian place of worship, but we bring together our different faiths today in a sign that there does not have to be enmity along political and religious lines, that we can learn to come together as members of a human family to ask that we may begin again. Because if the past days teach us anything it is that we fail and go on failing; we are truly human, with feet of clay.

'And we come here today too because we know it is by no means all over. Eric Semple is still missing, and no word of his whereabouts has been heard. So we are here too to pray for his safe return. There was new violence on the outskirts of Sudburgh last night with further casualties, and at this time we do not know if that situation has been brought under control. Many feel under the shadow of fear, on all sides of our rainbow community. All we can do this morning is to join together as one and ask for our Maker's forgiveness, and for guidance on the way ahead.

'I want to tell you about one of the victims of the horrendous bloodshed this Saturday. Every word of his story is true because I was there; I saw it with my own eyes. We had been warned by the police that there were certain parts of Sudburgh we should not visit; it felt as though we were almost told not to go out at all after dark. I had to say that such orders, or quasi-orders, bring out the worst in me. I am a woman and I have worked in war situations in Africa. I have learned that there are times when it is not worth waiting for the right person to do the job: it is best to do it yourself. And having listened, as I'm sure you did, to news updates through the hours, and having seen some of the live pictures from the city centre, I felt paralysed. So when I heard that we were being advised not to go out, or told not to – however you interpret what was said – I just sat there to begin with. I was numb as most of us were numb. And then I thought of a man I had come to know in recent months. He lived in a tower block, four flights up, and on a number of occasions we had met to talk; in other words, I had sought him out and we had talked. He was from Afghanistan and he had fled the country after his family was massacred by insurgents. He had learned English by listening to a radio, literally by pressing it to his ear through the night to learn a little, bit by bit. He had a beautiful voice; he spoke softly and slowly, because he knew that he was still learning. And at last he had been granted permission to come to England. He had lost everything when the insurgents destroyed his village; he arrived with almost nothing.

'I used to go to visit this quiet man because I knew that he had met God. I saw that in his eyes and heard it in his heart. I went to visit him not because I felt sorrow for an asylum seeker (though that was why I went there in the beginning). I went to find him because I recognised his wisdom and I left again with many wise words. He was only thirty-four, but somehow he had lived long beyond his years. But I wanted also to be a friend to him because I knew that he had had dog mess pushed through his letterbox and paint sprayed on his walls. I knew that a warning white rose had been put on his door, a sign that he was in danger of being attacked, that he had been earmarked. I prayed with him and he prayed with me, even though we came from different religious worlds and believed many different things. I can truly say he was one of the best men I ever met, and in saying that I think of all those I knew at theological college, and all those I encountered at conferences and retreat days and services for the great and the good in cathedrals. This man was one of the best I ever met.

'And so, at ten o'clock on Saturday night, I did one of the bravest or the most foolish things I've ever done – depending on your point of view. I went out to see that he was all right. And he lived in one of the districts we were told in no uncertain terms we should avoid. And to crown it all, I even walked there. It was, as I have said, that rebel within me that did not want to be told what to do, even though I probably knew what was best.

'The odd thing is that I met nobody, not on the walk there. It was eerie, but I could hear things far away: the sounds of shouting, the breaking of glass, the distant sound of what I think was someone being beaten. I don't deny that I was afraid; I think I even felt I should turn back more than once. I felt as though I was on the edge of a war; not that I was in one – that I was on the edge of one. But I most certainly felt that a war was going on.

'When I got to my friend's door, I saw that there was no need to knock. It wouldn't have been possible to knock. It looked as though someone had taken an axe to the door; it had then been torn from its hinges and thrown to one side. There was no sign of life from inside, no sound when I called. I knocked on a wall before softly padding in; the curtains weren't drawn and a certain amount of neon light filtered in from the windows at the back.

'And I found my friend in the living room, in a pool of his own blood. He had been stabbed no fewer than seventy-six times: that was what they established on the Sunday morning when his body was finally examined at the hospital. And I will never forget crouching there beside him in the darkness. I could see his face in the half-light of the room, and I crouched there in his blood. It was shining; that pool of blood was shining. And as I crouched there I thought that even then they could not take his shining from him. They could do everything to him, and in the end they took away his life, but they could not take his shining. And the strange thing is that I did not cry; I have not cried until now for his loss. I walked all the way back home and thought of that, of all the shining that cannot be taken away.'

★

A FTER WE CAME back upstairs, the three of us, I was still in shock. I think actually we all were: I suspect that what had happened was the last thing my superior expected. In a way of course it did him a mammoth favour, because what had he been planning on doing with the guy otherwise? If you announce publicly that all four bombers are dead, you can't suddenly produce one of them and say you made a counting error. And you certainly can't do it when you've tortured him. So it was the last thing he had thought of, but it was the best possible way out for him.

I remember none of us said a word on the stairs; I can remember the sound of our shoes *slipping* on the stone stairs. I don't really mean slipping, but I can't find a better word to describe the sound. That sound of shoes on smooth stone. I can't remember in what order we went back up and it doesn't seem to matter much now, but I do know that none of us said a word. Total silence. And I remember looking down before we got to the top and seeing the guy white in the darkness. It was very, very eerie. He was so white in the darkness. It was like a body that's been dug out of ancient ground, out of peat. He looked somehow like a fossil. And I thought of all that had happened.

My superior, my boss – call him what you will – went straight over to the interview room when we went back into the modern part of the building. He started sorting sheets of paper; he seemed completely himself. He clicked shut the little suitcase he had brought with him.

I just stood there, on one side of the table. The one thing he never did that whole time was look at me. I wanted to know what he was thinking; I somehow wanted to know whether or not all this had been worthwhile. I didn't want to know whether it was right or wrong; the philosophical discussion could wait for another time. But I wanted to know if it had been worthwhile.

I can't honestly recall what I said, what I asked. It was just the two of us there in the interview room – I don't know where my colleague was at that point. I was somehow irritated that all my superior could do was sort through papers. It seemed to be the last thing that mattered. So I suppose that's exactly what I did ask: if it had been worthwhile, if it had all served any purpose.

I couldn't believe the way he answered; you could almost hear the shrug of his shoulders in the way he replied. Of course it had been worthwhile; there had been mention of the base at Faslane. I knew that was where the nuclear submarines were stationed on the Clyde, but I had never heard the word *Faslane* actually mentioned. Of course it was worthwhile, he said again – this would mean the place could be ring-fenced and any possible attack prevented.

I just didn't know what to say to that and so I didn't say anything. I can remember feeling rather foolish; I felt very much as though I had been written out of everything. He was still going on tidying papers and I found myself asking what would happen to the body. I remember he smiled at that. He assured me everything would be taken

care of as far as that was concerned. There was absolutely
nothing to be worried about there.

★

I WAS GIVEN a letter to take to his wife. I used to go
there every day to give him food and water. I still
don't want to reveal the locations where he was kept. I
believe to do so might put people in jeopardy even now.
I don't want that risk to be taken. Thank you. One was
a cellar, that I can say. He was kept there partly because
the police were searching everywhere over those days.
I have many friends who experienced dawn raids; their
children were terrified because armed police broke in to
search the house. I think they kept on being sure they had
found the right place. The idea was also that he should
know something of the conditions of prisoners who had
been held and interrogated by the CIA; I think especially
those who were victims of rendition. And he was moved
several times. How many? I'm not sure; I think I saw
him in three different places. He was always kept in a
tiny room, a cell, that had been specially made for hiding
him. They were dark and certainly cold. But it was very
hot outside; it was the height of the summer so in fact
it was cool there rather than cold. Usually he would be

moved without warning in the middle of the night; he would be blindfolded and taken out, driven to the new location. I am not going to give any of the names: that is impossible. That is not why I agreed to speak today. I wanted only to read the letter.

How did I find him? I must say he was very kind; I do not remember him being angry or desperate to escape. He seemed calm and perhaps resigned. I felt sorry that he was chained like an animal. There was nothing I could do or say; I was there only to bring food and water. I was not supposed to say a word, to speak to him at all. No, I did not – I knew that I was not to speak and so I did not. But I did smile at him and I did not think this was wrong. Did I feel unhappy at his condition? I am not sure. I think it is true to say that part of me did feel unhappy. But he was also there for a reason. He had been kidnapped and imprisoned for a reason. If there had not been a reason I would have felt more unhappy. No, I did not know what was going to happen. I did not ask and I was not told. I have said they wanted him to know what it was like to be imprisoned, that is all. But yes, there was fear he might be found – that is why he was moved from one place to another several times. Yes, the letter.

One day he put into my hand a piece of crumpled paper. He had one hand free; the left one was always chained to the wall. It was a completely crumpled piece of paper, a ball, and at first I had no idea what it was – if I thought of anything, I imagined it was just rubbish. But he said to me very quietly to take it, that it was a letter for his wife. He begged me to take it, pushed it into my hand. I had put down the bowl of water so my hands were empty. I didn't know what to do, but I stayed; no one else was there at that time. He said the address was on the letter; I would find the address there. Please would I take it to his wife, and he begged me several times. He kept thanking me.

What did I do with it? I had to hide it when I came home; I did not know what else to do with it. I hid it in a box at the back of a cupboard. Yes, I was frightened that my husband might find it. He would have been angry.

Why did I not take it to his wife? I did think of it. I lay awake the first night, still wondering what I should do. I knew that I should take it; I did want to help him. I was not saving his life or revealing where he was hidden. Yes, I had read the letter myself before I hid it, before my husband came home. It was an innocent letter; there was no reason to be suspicious of it. And the address was there on the paper. So I drove there, perhaps the next day or the day after. I felt guilty because I was going behind my husband's back. But I saw at once it would have been impossible. The police were everywhere. I can remember that they looked at me as I drove past. How could I give the letter to them? They would have arrested me at once or questioned me. And I did know where he was being hidden. No, I was not at all tempted to tell them. Was that because I believed it was right he was being held captive or because I was afraid? I am not sure how to answer your question. I do not think it was a choice for me. I do not believe I felt there was any choice at all at that moment.

So I kept the letter, hidden where I have told you. I thought about it many times; I did not forget about it. I have not forgotten about it to this day. Why did I decide to give it now? The answer is that I wanted to. I think it is about being brave and honest. Many people are telling things that were secret. No, I am not afraid. I do not know what my husband will say. But I will read the letter. I have said everything else, so I will read the letter:

My love –

I don't have long to write this; they'll be back in a few minutes. I found a stub of pencil and some paper in an inside pocket – no idea how I'll get it to you, but I'll try. No idea where I am either; this is the third place. Most of all I want to say I'm sorry. None of this would have happened if I had gone on with things as they were. I can imagine what it's like for you and the kids right now, but I want you to know I love you. We had the best time. I sit down here remembering, all the good things. There's nothing to regret and don't give up. Whatever you do, don't give up.

Eric

★

I WAS ONE of the police out looking for Semple; that's
the simplest way of introducing myself. I'm originally
from London, been in the North for about ten years now, I
suppose. It was a horrible time; in fact, it's what made me
leave the police. I just didn't want to be part of the force
any more; didn't like what we had to do – hammering
on people's doors and searching properties. The whole
atmosphere was horrible. It was hot; you couldn't sleep
at night; you were remembering hearing children crying
and people screaming at you. I just realised I wasn't cut
out for it any more; by the end of those weeks I felt a
nervous wreck. My wife and I were unhappy; the kids
were miserable. I just wasn't myself; I didn't want to
come home at night. I felt I was someone else, that I was
acting in the wrong play. All of it felt wrong.

I just felt it was an 'us and them' situation. I felt we
were two different worlds. It was like two men shouting
at each other from two different cliffs and neither
hearing what the other said. And you both just go on
shouting. We were doing the politicians' dirty work for
them. They don't get their hands dirty. That's another
reason I left. I think I really saw that for the first time. It
wasn't achieving anything. All we were doing was alien-
ating people. I mean, what good does it do hammering
on someone's door, bursting your way in, shouting at
everyone and turning the place upside-down? And
leaving again having found not a bloody thing? Tell me
what the point is, what that achieves.

Of course there was a reason for what we were doing;

I know that! But I simply don't think it helped solve anything. It didn't bring Eric Semple back; I doubt very much it prevented more unrest. I can only think it would have been counter-productive. I know, it's easy for me to say all this now I'm out. I certainly felt it, but I wouldn't have voiced it. I bottled it up. That's why things were so unhappy at home. No doubt about it.

There was one day I saw this little girl, she would have been four, four and a half. We had gone in somewhere, two of us, and I was at the back. There was this little girl frightened over in the corner. She had thick dark curls and she was hiding her face. I was closest to her and I could see she was trembling. I tell you what I thought afterwards: it sounds crazy, but what I wanted to do was freeze everything. To freeze the whole scene except for me and that little girl. I just wanted to go over and kneel down and tell her it would be all right. And I didn't; I couldn't. We had to go on shouting, even though there was nothing to shout about and we solved nothing.

I didn't go home that evening, not until much later. I didn't even phone my wife to tell her where I was or what I was doing. I had just come to the end of everything. I was in no fit state to drive my own car, but I did. I went out of Sudburgh and I was driving towards these slate-grey skies. It was totally airless outside, oppressively hot. The edges of the sky were all pink, this strange orange-pink. I don't know what I was thinking; in a way I was trying not to think at all. I was seeing that little girl and what we had done, and I couldn't get it out of my head.

And I parked in this layby and I sort of half realised I didn't know where the hell I was. There was sun coming from one side, low and gold, and ahead of me was this wall of black. It was scary. It was like something out of a film, like the beginning of the end of the world. And I just cried; I just cried for I don't know how long. I think it's the first real time I've cried as a grown man. I didn't even cry at my dad's funeral.

I wasn't just crying for that little girl; I felt I was crying for myself. I didn't know who I was any more and I didn't like myself; I didn't like who I had become. And then the storm broke and I had the best seat in the house. The whole sky cracked open and it rained; it rained so the ground hissed. And I got out and stood in it for a long time and it felt so good. My face was washed by the rain and it felt like a kind of healing. And I drove back in and I knew that that was it. I wasn't going to do this any more; I was going to leave. I didn't care what anyone said. That little girl had made me see myself.

★

THE LEADER OF the right-wing extremist group White Rose has been found dead in the Peak District after having been reported missing from his home two days ago.

There had been mounting pressure on Andrew Gregory after the violence that followed the march through Sudburgh city centre in memory of Terry Radcliffe and in protest at the kidnapping of Eric Semple. Police had been searching a sector of the Peak District after a tip-off from a senior member of White Rose. They say they are not seeking anyone else in connection with Andrew Gregory's death.

The hunt for Eric Semple has been stepped up yet again, with more officers being drafted in from neighbouring towns to scour disused buildings and to make door-to-door enquiries. Police say those enquiries have been hampered by the sheer level of anger felt against the white community in the wake of the Sudburgh march. Asian community leaders continue to complain that not nearly enough has been done to make members of their communities feel safe amid what they describe as a toxic atmosphere in Sudburgh. But a spokesman for White Rose said there was little chance of the white community feeling safe when even newly elected members of parliament were dragged from their own houses. There are renewed calls for the Prime Minister to visit Sudburgh and to speak to representatives from both sides of the divide, but Downing Street continues to insist that what matters is for local solutions to be found through local dialogue. However, political activists in Sudburgh have stressed again today that the longer the Prime Minister puts off a visit, the worse things will become. It is likely that mounting pressure will see a visit from the Home Secretary; he has asked

for cool heads and patient hearts, saying that the pressure
on the Prime Minister in recent days and weeks has been
all but intolerable.

★

I THINK BACK on it now and reckon everything started
with those four from Manchester. They set in motion
the whole thing. You know those stupid trails they used
to set up on television, where an egg rolled down a ledge
into a teaspoon, and that set off a ball along a tube, and
so on and so on – it was like that. And the crazy thing is
that those four had no idea what they were doing. I'm not
calling them innocent; I'm doing anything but calling
them innocent. I've called them things I've called no one
in my life. And because of what they set in motion. That's
where White Rose really started. It might have begun
beforehand, but that's where they got their recruits. That
and the fact that not one solitary soul was ever arrested.
How d'you think that makes people feel? It's somehow
worth arresting even one individual, just to release them
again in a week's time. Citizens want answers when
a train full of innocent people is bombed off the rails.
This isn't Afghanistan or Iraq. This is supposed to be
somewhere that sort of thing just doesn't happen, where

it's not allowed to happen. And it's not enough to make a garden of remembrance and hope the whole thing will be forgotten. That was the spark; that was the first real flame.

I'm a teacher and I saw kids crying openly that morning; they sat on benches in the foyer and cried. Boys of sixteen, seventeen. They felt scared, shattered. We're a post-religious society and what do we have to offer them? Nothing. I felt that morning we had nothing to offer them but listening ears. It was just the same the Monday after the battle in Sudburgh. Several kids said to me they were ashamed to be British. They looked at me and said that from their hearts. And I nodded, because I understood and could only agree with them.

And suddenly we're here in the middle of a war. It's not a war where I teach; it's a quiet suburb on the edge of Manchester. But you feel there's a war all the same, almost underground. You can't see it or hear it, but you can sense it underground. And the war could be at the next bus station, on the top floor of that block of flats, in that car parked by the side of the road. It's a war that's watching and waiting all the time, and it'll be back when you least expect it and were sure it was gone for good. It gives me no pleasure to say that, but it's true, and if you don't believe it then I think you're burying your head. And it all began with four people who didn't have a clue what they were setting in motion. And they never did know because they blew themselves sky-high. At least that's what we were told at the time.

But who really knows what to believe. Who knows that either any more.

★

I DON'T FEEL there is much to say. It happened very early in the morning, in a place where we have met before. It is chosen for secrecy. I would say that we are using Sharia law; I would not describe it as a Sharia court. Yes, I have been involved in many such cases before, not only here but in other places, too. Most of them in the north of England.

Yes, he was given a chance to speak but he chose to say very little. He was kept at the front; I could not see him because I imagine he would have been kneeling and I was at the back. I think he was on trial for the hatred he had stirred up against the Asian community, particularly in Sudburgh but far more widely. No, I do not believe he was being charged with any actual attacks. But he was being held responsible for stirring up a great deal of hatred in white communities; you could say he was being charged with radicalising young people in particular.

Do I accept that he was being made a scapegoat? Well, I did not think of it like that at the time, and I don't know if I do so now. It is true there was a lot of anger, a sense that the violence had gone in one direction. More than that there was an anger against the police. We knew there was racism within the police, even though that was not accepted and was never dealt with. We lived with it on a daily basis. For some people, I don't think there seemed much difference between White Rose and the police. They were both to be feared. I do not say that about all the police. There was an element. And we did not feel enough had been done after the Sudburgh march. That was a terrible day for us. These were attacks by thugs. Look at the numbers of those who were killed and injured. Of course there was a desire for revenge. And now the police were breaking down Asian doors to find out where their racist hero was being kept! They were not breaking down white doors to find the ones who had committed brutal crimes that Saturday afternoon! So tell me, who would not be angry and who would not want revenge?

You are asking again if I believe he was a scapegoat. Was there a sense of triumph that we had got him and would it have been impossible to release him alive? I was only one of the representatives who were there that day. Yes, I suppose it was a trial. It is not for me to decide if it was fair or unfair. He had given himself to a cause of hatred and that was how he was being judged. Look at the manner in which this country has treated our radical preachers again and again. Consider the hatred that this one man had stirred up against us. No, he did not commit violent crimes himself, but he was more than content for others to carry them out in his name. That was what he wanted. That was his intention. He might have denied it to the end, but I believe it was his objective. He was not cruelly treated during the time he was held; there was no attempt made to get information out of him at any point. So I think this was a just trial. It was conducted in our way and not in yours, that is the problem. Well, you can have me arrested now that you have got me. You can enjoy the superiority of your British criminal justice system! There are reasons that we believe in Sharia law. It is not about being cruel and barbaric, as Eric Semple and White Rose would want to claim. It is about a true sense of justice, a justice for victims. I believe that is something you have lost sight of. I realise it is not the criminal justice system that is on trial today; I realise that in many ways it is me. That is what it feels like, let me tell you.

As I said at the beginning, I have little to say. I believe that Eric Semple condemned himself. There was no sign of remorse, no hint of guilt for the hatred he had wanted to raise against the Asian community as a whole. That is all I have to say.

★

I THINK ONE thing that is forgotten in all this is the sheer division between the north and south of England.

And I'm saying that to you as someone who was born and bred in Kent. But I spent many years in the North too; I had the grave misfortune to be born a Catholic and packed off to a boarding school for boys – it had better remain nameless – at the tender age of eight. I thought I had died and gone to hell, except for the fact that hell was made up of moorland and eternally grey skies, and some rather dubious housemasters. But the truth is that a hell of a lot of those who're in positions of power in the South really know very little about the modus vivendi of the North. They spend a lot of time trying to pretend they do, but I'm afraid I'm pretty cynical about that at the best of times. They don't actually terribly like the idea of the North, but they think they have a vague notion of what goes on there. I know that sounds straight out of a rather poor and hackneyed comedy, but for a good number, for all too many – it simply is the truth.

London is an addiction. It just is its own planet, and if you're on the power ladder you don't want to leave, and in the end you can't leave. I think of countless men who've succumbed to London. It's funny, I think of men first and foremost, and I don't believe I've ever properly considered that before.

But to get back to the start of all this, I do believe a lot of the crisis (and I really do use that word intentionally), was about the sheer divide between North and South. That mess was allowed to grow more toxic by the day in the North, while those in the Westminster Bubble looked on and did nothing. They did nothing at all! Now

I emphasise that as far as the panic over Sudburgh was concerned, there *was* no easy solution. It was somehow too late by then. But the fact is that it was all allowed to fester for so long before there was even *talk* about what might be done to remedy things. And some of that is purely and simply, believe me, because it was *oop north*, it was far away. Few things have made me angrier in my parliamentary career – and heaven knows that's taken a long time and a great number of so-called crises. And have we learned? Well, I suspect we have learned a bit from all this – God help us if we haven't – but I don't believe the two halves of England are much better glued together. I'm sorry to sound so old and grumpy on that score, but I think I have good reason to be concerned. England's a very broken country.

★

I REMEMBER IT being a beautiful Sunday morning in Sudburgh. I woke up before six and the sky was just a single pane of blue. I remember crouching at the windowsill looking out. One plane crossed the sky and there was no sound from it and the trail turned this vibrant pure orange. The whole trail fluffed out the way they do, and for the first time in my life I saw an inherent beauty there. I realised I wasn't going to get back to sleep and I wanted to go out, and then I thought of everything that had happened in recent days. And I felt quite angry. I felt angry that I shouldn't be able to just go outside and enjoy the morning. I'm not a religious person; I'm not religious in the least. But that was somehow what I felt: that I was being denied the right to go out and experience that morning, just for what it was. And that was why I *did* go out in the end.

I don't even like describing myself as white. When you grow up here that feels like a loaded term, especially now. *White* feels like a clenched fist; it feels like a statement of defiance. All the labels we have for one another, all the ways we have of defining ourselves. I feel an individual. I'm a person with dreams and doubts and a past and a future, and the amazing thing is that never before has there been someone quite like me, nor will there be again. I know that's going to sound like quasi-religious bullshit, or something like it. It's going to sound so narcissistic and I'm fully aware of that. But it matters all the same. To get beyond that place where labels matter.

I have a garden at the back of this little house. I was looking out over it when I woke up before six and knelt at the window ledge to watch the plane. Somehow that garden and what I feel so deeply about being free are linked, and I can't for the life of me begin to explain that. The garden is tiny; it's just a circle of ground surrounded by trees and high walls.

When I first moved here I had depression. I don't

mean that I was down now and again; I suffered real clinical depression. I can't remember now how many pills I took every day. Twelve or fourteen, something like that. I rarely went out; I sat at this window and thought of nothing. It was like I was wrapped in cotton wool. I wasn't even unhappy; I was just numb. I've no idea where I saw the picture of the pond. No, that's not true – it was in an underpass, a concrete underpass. I was walking through and stopped to look at it; it was about the first thing I had paid any attention to in months. It showed a pond with reeds, and there was this dragonfly fluttering up above. It was the colours that stopped me. Everything had been grey for so long and here were these blues and greens and golds. I can't say what it meant; it's impossible to convey.

But I went back and I went straight out to the garden. It was crazy; I started digging with my bare hands in the lawn. It's just as well no one saw me; they'd have come to take me away. The thing was that the ground was awful; I mean, it was full of builders' rubbish. There were old bits of wire and glass and brick; even after I got my tools for digging I can remember cutting my hands over and over again. But somehow it didn't matter. I would keep thinking of what I'd seen painted on the wall of that underpass, those colours that meant more than anything, that stayed in my head.

And I'll never forget the day I let the water flow over the lining to fill that pond. I got moss to grow up the sides to hide the ugly edges of the lining; I wanted to make it as real as I could. I used to get up early to go out

141

and work there, long before the rush hour. And I felt better than I had done in years; my heart felt as if it was singing. My hands actually used to shake, but not with fear – with sheer joy and excitement. This was mine; I had made it myself and it was my very own little Eden.

That's all I did that morning of the beautiful jet trail. I went down into the garden and I crouched by the side of the pond. It was a Sunday morning and there simply wasn't a sound in the city. And I was thinking of all that had happened, of all this crazy fighting over the past days and how it was quiet at last. And as I've said, I'm not religious; I'm not in the least religious, but I found myself praying it would stay that way, that it would be over. So it somehow wasn't a selfish happiness, it wasn't just about having found a place that was beyond labels. It was about more than that. It was about being one of the people, too. And maybe that showed there had been a kind of healing as well, the fact that I wasn't just curled into myself and content with that. It's the only time I've prayed in my life.

★

I USED TO go there from time to time. It was close to the block where I lived, only about ten minutes away, if it was as far as that. There was a way of getting through an old wall that stood between the wasteland and the field on the other side. It was quicker than going by the road – and safer. It's also something about not being seen by people; when you're a heroin addict you know what people think of you. You know how they look at you and you feel that.

I've moved from the area now and I'm actually getting treatment; I've been off drugs for about three months now. But that summer was bad; I couldn't sleep properly, partly because of the heat, and I had trouble finding a good supplier. Your whole life is about one thing: guaranteeing the next fix. I was on my own; I'd had a partner for about six years and she was an addict, too. I'm ashamed to say I don't even know what happened to her. I can't begin to describe the state of the flat we had in that block. It was just a drug den. Over the weekend there might be ten or twelve people staying there. The floor was covered in bottles, cigarette ends, everything. The place just stank. You didn't really care who was there and who wasn't. If they had something you needed or wanted that was all that mattered. Your whole world collapses in on that. You really end up caring about nobody but yourself. It's as sad as that.

The block was mainly made up of Pakistanis; they were mostly all Asian at any rate. I was on the top floor so I'd pass them going up and down. I can't remember saying very much; if I was going out it was usually because I was on the hunt for something I needed and was desperate. The last thing on my mind was seeing someone on the stairs. And I've said I also felt aware of what they'd think of me. I had lost a lot of weight and must have looked terrible; my clothes had burn marks. I just remember one old woman greeting me on the stairs when I met her; I'm sure I often passed her and didn't even see her properly. But she always smiled and if I cared enough to smile back then I would.

But over that summer I seem to remember the flat being almost empty. My partner had left and I don't even remember her leaving. It was more a case of her going and then not actually coming back. I was very sick and I had these terrible dreams. I was frightened of going to sleep because I'd keep waking up with these hellish night-mares. It was a vicious circle because I was exhausted from the night before; I'd try to keep myself awake on the sofa, drift off and wake up in a cold sweat. So I used to go out walking through the night, just anywhere. I felt sick and I'd be shivering, but it was better than those hours on the sofa with this trail of nightmares. The flat was too hot anyway; even through the night it was too hot. I was on the top floor and the place was boiling during the day; you had twelve hours of sunlight, and it was a baking summer. You couldn't have the windows open through the night because of the risk of people getting in. It wasn't a good area and people could climb up onto the balcony if they really wanted to. I'm sure my windows were open through the night all the same; I just wouldn't have cared or remembered. But the place was usually totally airless...

I'd wake up from one of those nightmares, gasping for breath, and I felt I couldn't get enough air into my lungs. I felt I was breathing cotton wool. That was another reason for wanting to get out.

I had a vague sense that something was wrong in Sudburgh. Yeah, I know it must sound highly amusing and you're welcome to laugh, but I'm afraid that was as far as it went. If somebody had sat me down and explained the situation I couldn't have cared less; I'd have shrugged my shoulders. If it had affected my heroin supply I'd have bothered – it's as simple as that. So the only thing I knew was that I'd gone to this place to sit through the last of the night. It was sort of half-underground; there were steps down and you went inside this kind of concrete shelter. The kids used to go there on Saturday nights, some of the really young ones especially. It was away through this waste ground and on the edge of a field; it was just dark and smelly, but it was a kind of a hide-out. As far as I was concerned it was simply somewhere to sit. I would just crouch there and hug myself, rock backwards and forwards. All I wanted was to keep the nightmares out.

I have no idea what the time was when I was in there; I just know it would have been the middle of the night. I felt sick but I couldn't be sick; I was knackered but I was too scared to go to sleep. I was glad to be out of the flat but I felt awful. I think I even knew I couldn't go down much further. I think I was frightened by that, because I had no idea what I was going to do. I didn't have a clue about finding an answer.

All I remember is that it started to get light. I was sitting right at the back of the place, as far into the shadows as I could get. There was a sort of step in front of me; I'm not sure how to describe it other than that. It was quite high and it was made of solid concrete, like the rest of the place. There was just that greyness you get before dawn; it was nothing like fully light. And I was looking ahead of me at that step, and I realised there was something on it. There was something standing on it; I could see the shape in the half-light.

It could have been anything; the place was really not much more than a kind of rubbish dump. It could have been a burst football that someone had chucked in; it was about that kind of size. But it wasn't that and it began to get more and more light. I knew I was going to have to go; I didn't want to be found there and I staggered to my feet in the end. I was sick and dizzy; I can still remember how terrible I felt. I wanted to die; I wanted nothing more than to die. I was drawn by that thing, that shape, and I sort of swam forward over the ground. It was still too dark to see the concrete below; there was just this greyness about the ledge.

I got there in the end and I bent right down to see what it was. And I screamed; it was like something from the worst of my nightmares. It was a head, the head of a man. And the eyes were looking at me, open and looking

146

at me, even though they were dead. And I vomited; I was
sick until my guts were empty.

★

I WON'T FORGET that vigil. I'm housebound and over
eighty, and I tend to go to bed about nine. I was just
drawing the curtains and I saw them gathering. I live
right above the city centre, have a view all the way along
the main streets. I knew what this was about right away.
I live by the radio and have done for forty years, since
the day my wife Janice died. I knew they had found
Eric Semple and guessed they would be gathering to
remember him. Poor man; may he rest in peace. No one
deserves to die like that.

I was afraid it would spark a riot. I thought we would
be back to square one, with hundreds of those White
Rose activists marching and setting fire to anything and
anyone Asian. That had been a frightening day, the day
of the march and what it became. I watched hours of it
from here, until I grew too afraid to watch any more. I
went to bed and cowered. I didn't sleep and listened to
it for hours through the night. That was a lynch mob. I
didn't ever believe I'd see something like that in England.
I was once in the Deep South of America, in the days

147

when Janice was still alive, and you felt the tension – you could cut it like a knife. I didn't ever think it could be like that here, but I was wrong. It's easy enough to destroy something; much harder to put it back together. I don't think that'll happen in my lifetime.

But the night they found Eric Semple, the night of the vigil, it was almost eerie. They just gathered, hundreds and hundreds of people. I suppose it's what they call social media; there had been no mention of anything on the radio – not a word. But the riot police were there too, and they were there in force. They had got a hell of a rap over the knuckles for the last time; they weren't going to make that mistake again. It looked as if all the side streets were cordoned off; the vigil was contained in one space, right at the city's heart. But I don't believe they'd come for violence, that's the strange thing. I'm sure half of Sudburgh was afraid of a riot and the other half had left already. But I couldn't have been more wrong. There were no loudspeakers, no chanting – I don't even remember seeing banners. Perhaps they had said something on the internet, told them what they wanted it to be. I suppose before they had been marching in fury because Eric Semple had been kidnapped; no one had a clue where he was and White Rose felt they had been beaten. Now it was all over. There was no amount of rioting would bring him back. There was actually a bit of trouble much later in the night; what you might call a small pocket of violence. But at that vigil someone just sang and the place was white with candles. I suppose that was deliberate. I remember I had tears in my eyes. I had no great love for Semple, but who would wish a death like that on their worst enemy? And what had his last days been like? There was no need for that. I cried as much for his family. I cried as much for them as for him. But may he rest in peace.

★

'THANK YOU FOR coming here so early in the morning. I decided to speak to the country from Downing Street, and I finally made that decision late last night. I don't need to tell any of you how ghastly the past weeks have been. Many of you will have watched the news footage and wondered for a moment if you were watching a film. But it has been real, all of it, and devastatingly so.

'I believed that after the Burroway bombing we might be able to recover, slowly but surely, and learn to move on. I see now that the bombing was a spark that ignited a bonfire. I believe the bonfire was set and ready and tinder dry; all that was needed was that one spark. What it unleased has been nothing less than nightmarish, and again and again it has been innocent members of communities on both sides of the divide who have suffered. In fact, it has been the ones in the middle, the ones who have not sought to be part of the conflict at all, who have been ensnared in it time and time again.

'And I have been accused of not caring, of being in some kind of ivory tower here in London. The accusations have come from fellow politicians – some of them in my own party – and from the police and the media and far beyond. It is not because of these accusations that I have made the decision I am announcing today. I am resigning as Prime Minister, and I do so with great regret and after much soul searching. I am resigning because I have come to the conclusion that I have failed. I am a lawyer and an economist, and if I was put at the helm of my party for any reason, then it was to champion the cause of the economy. And I am glad and proud that I resign as Prime Minister with that economy much stronger than when I came to office.

'But I accept that it is going to take strengths and skills I may not possess to put this country back together in a very different manner. One of our most eminent journalists has written that England is broken in the middle, but that no one quite knows where the break is or how to mend it. I think this mending process is going to take teachers and social workers and theologians and community activists, and perhaps the politicians will come at the end of that line. But I say that not as any excuse; I simply acknowledge that there are times when those of us who can mend broken economies have to admit when they can't mend broken countries.

'I established the Burroway Fund after the bombing, and I'm proud I did so. To date we have raised some four millions pounds, not only to help the families who suffered bereavement and injury, but also to support their communities. I want, for the time being at least, to leave the limelight and to work with the fund to develop its activities further. So I am not giving up on the task I have outlined; I am devoting myself to it in a more direct way. I want to thank all of those who have supported me over my years in office, and I want to say sorry to all of those I am letting down now. But I have looked deep into my soul and seen clearly what had to be said and what had to be done. And that is something for which no one should be ashamed. Thank you.'

★

I FOUND THE Prime Minister's speech quite nauseating, and I was one of his own backbenchers. He didn't even have the courage to stand and spout all this sanctimonious nonsense in Downing Street: he invited the cameras in and said the whole thing behind closed doors. Why? Because even then he was scared someone from either the Islamic world or from White Rose might take a pop at him. He was a quivering jelly, make no mistake.

But the killing of Eric Semple was just a good chance to run out the door marked exit. The truth is he had been looking for his moment for long enough. And the root cause? Nothing to do with White Rose or all his troubles in the North; it was all right at his own back door. He had been having an affair and his wife had found out; she was going to reveal all, and those closest to him in the party knew the whole story. He had been told to fall on his own sword before the party was let into that mess.

But there was another reason, too; the reasons were fighting to form an orderly queue at the door of Number 10. A policeman from the Met, high enough up the ladder, was all set to go to the tabloids with his story of the fourth bomber from Burroway. According to him the fourth man had survived and been kept at some secret location in London, then given the third degree to get as much out of him as possible. The tabloids had got out their chequebooks as they always do and were all set to pay him a small fortune for his story. The PM knew well enough there would be a hell of a rumpus over that. Not only was it likely to set off the extremists in the Islamic camp, it would lead to baying for a public inquiry. To be fair to him on that one, I think it came sailing out of a clear blue sky. I think that must have been the Met's little secret – until it was too tempting to keep it a secret any longer.

So quite frankly, I think most of us breathed something of a sigh of relief when he announced he was throwing in the towel. I got on fine and well with him in private;

he had a good-enough heart. But he was quite right: he didn't have the stamina. The paradox is that he may not actually have believed all that saccharine stuff about being an economist and not a healer, but it was absolutely true. I just think it was all the cloaks he was hiding behind that sickened us. Had he really *meant* what he said we might have respected him. No, the person we did respect in the end was Trish Semple. And she stood on her front step and said it. Twenty-four hours after her husband was found decapitated. Now that takes courage. The PM might have got some kind of Oscar for his performance. She got our admiration. And perhaps she did something to bridge that gulf between North and South. She did that night anyway. Without a shadow of a doubt.

★

'BUT FOR ALL that I don't feel hate. I think I've even tried to feel hate and failed. Perhaps hate, even for a time, might make things easier. Right now all I feel is nothingness, like at the end of a long road. I never truly believed that Eric would walk back alive through this front door. I knew he was too much of a prize for that, in the middle of a time of war. His murder was a way of getting revenge.

'Yet despite all the nothingness that I feel tonight, I don't want there to be any more revenge. I don't want there to be deaths in the name of Eric Semple, ever. I know Eric wouldn't have wanted that. He had strong views and he held those views with all his heart, but I don't ever remember hatred in him. He wanted change and he wanted fairness, and to the end he wanted people to think. But he didn't want them to hate, and he didn't want them to pour their hatred into killing. Maybe his biggest failing was not really knowing how much he stirred people up. I think I can say I knew Eric better than anyone, but I don't truly know if he was always aware of the effect he had on people.

'I've got the media here at my door tonight, because my husband was a kind of unelected leader of a movement. I've got the media at my door, too, let's face it, because he died a gruesome death and that makes the story all the more exciting. But all I want to say is that now it needs to be over. There have been enough deaths on both sides, and the deaths have got us nowhere. It's time to start sorting out the mess, not making the mess worse.

'I'm not going to say much more because I'm tired and I need time to be with my family and grieve. But let's look at all this brokenness tomorrow and start working out what went wrong. Don't let's start looking for more scapegoats; let's begin to understand where we went wrong ourselves.'

Publisher's Note

2020 is entirely a work of fiction, and all the characters are products of the author's imagination. Difficult though it may be to believe, the novel was not directly inspired either by the Brexit referendum or by the more recent events in Europe, the USA and around the world. It was in fact written largely in 2015 when, although simmering tensions and discontent were very much in the air, such dramatic societal upheavals still seemed to most of us highly unlikely. Thus, 2020 is not a response to Brexit. Rather, it is an eerily prescient expression of the mood of a nation divided.